Russ,

May the words in ___
of encouragement in your walk wi___
the Lord.

Joel N___

Romans 12:2

STOP
CALLING ME
CHRISTIAN

Discovering the True Gospel of Jesus

JOSH NELSON

WESTBOW
PRESS®
A DIVISION OF THOMAS NELSON
& ZONDERVAN

Scripture taken from the NEW AMERICAN STANDARD BIBLE®, Copyright © 1960, 1962, 1963, 1968, 1971, 1972, 1973, 1975, 1977, 1995 by The Lockman Foundation. Used by permission.

THE HOLY BIBLE, NEW INTERNATIONAL VERSION®, NIV® Copyright © 1973, 1978, 1984, 2011 by Biblica, Inc.® Used by permission. All rights reserved worldwide.

Scripture quotations marked (NLT) are taken from the Holy Bible, New Living Translation, copyright © 1996, 2004, 2007 by Tyndale House Foundation. Used by permission of Tyndale House Publishers, Inc., Carol Stream, Illinois 60188. All rights reserved.

Scripture taken from the King James Version of the Bible.

Scripture taken from The Message. Copyright © 1993, 1994, 1995, 1996, 2000, 2001, 2002. Used by permission of NavPress Publishing Group.

WestBow Press books may be ordered through booksellers or by contacting:

WestBow Press
A Division of Thomas Nelson & Zondervan
1663 Liberty Drive
Bloomington, IN 47403
www.westbowpress.com
1 (866) 928-1240

ISBN: 978-1-9736-4480-4 (sc)
ISBN: 978-1-9736-4481-1 (hc)
ISBN: 978-1-9736-4479-8 (e)

Library of Congress Control Number: 2018913346

Print information available on the last page.

WestBow Press rev. date: 11/14/2018

CONTENTS

ACKNOWLEDGMENTS

Without the love from God that shines through others, this book would not have been possible.

To my incredible and loving parents, Larry and Gayle Nelson
You named me prophetically in the same name of our Lord. Thank you for teaching me along your own journey and walk with Jesus. Mom, your dedication to your study of scripture and commitment to teach me the Jesus you know has made an indelible mark on me. I will forever stand up before others and call you "blessed." You have never been too busy to take time to listen and love. Your selflessness for others, especially your family, is something I aspire to have. Dad, you have never been ashamed of your Lord and Savior Jesus Christ before others. Your willingness to share your testimony before many is the earliest memory I have of the gospel. You have modeled throughout your life an unmatched humility in the light of worldly success. You lead in actions above words. Your life has been a constant sermon to many, including me. I thank you for not clouding your sermon with unneeded words. You allowed me to grow in Jesus, and you always trusted him with me in his hands.

To my sweet bride, Kimberly
You have taught me of the tenderness of God since the first day I met you. Your unconditional support of my pursuit of Jesus is matchless, and your heart is too beautiful for words. When I start to

feel shortchanged in any way by God, all I have to do is look at the life partner he gave me and realize that I am a truly blessed man. I do not deserve you, but it's too late now for me to convince you of that. So I will love you and cherish you forever.

To my sons, Caleb and Noah

May you one day read this book and see through any faults of mine as your father and know who I am committed to become more like. May you grow in wisdom and stature in the way of Jesus. I am proud of you! You are God's creation; I pray that you will know him intimately and make him known. He knit you together in your mother's womb and designed you with purpose. I offer you both to him.

To Kerie Brown

Though you had no clue of the life-changing impact of the words you spoke to me one evening in our junior year of college, thank you for speaking the truth in love. You were a messenger of God.

To Tom Randall

To this day you are still the best representation I have ever seen of Jesus in today's culture. I have never seen you waver from his call on your life. Thank you for modeling the abundant life in Jesus that is so infectious to so many around the world, including me. I aspire to be more like you.

To Cole Forsyth

Your friendship means the world to me. Thank you for challenging me to never stop growing in my faith through spending time alone with the Lord in scripture. The milestones of my journey in Christ would not be where they are without your encouragement and devotion.

To Jim Hiskey

Thank you for being the first person to ever truly walk alongside me with no agenda other than that of a disciple of Jesus. I will never forget that the person I need to disciple the most is me. Because of you, I will forever be a better disciple-maker.

To Andy Stanley

I have sat in your congregation for more than sixteen years. I have listened and relistened to probably just about every sermon you have ever given (at least since they were recorded). You have poured into much of my spiritual journey without ever knowing it. You inspire me to grow into a great communicator of truth.

To my ministry partners at Links Players International

Thank you for allowing me to grow and serve alongside you for the last eight years. You have encouraged and supported my progression as a follower of Jesus, minister, and writer. Keep up the good work. You are all "changing the conversation."

This book was written in special memory of my grandparents, Julia and Ray Harrison and Rudell and Vernon Nelson, and my father-in-law, Larry Sapp, I look forward to being reunited with each of you for eternity.

Part 1

I do not know for sure if I was born with my life-threatening condition or contracted it at a very young age; regardless, early in my life I contracted a disease that leads to the most common form of blindness in America. This ailment usually comes on without any recognition and increases in severity before it is ever detected. A malady that has blinded people for centuries unfortunately gets very little attention because it is very hard to diagnose. Thankfully, I had a very perceptive friend in college, the daughter of an accomplished pediatric surgeon, who recognized its symptoms during my junior year. Thankfully, she was not afraid to point it out. I don't know where I'd be today without this God-sent friend—likely permanently blind and living in a dark, hopeless place, suffering from Christian *Phariseeism*.

We have great historical documentation about the Phariseeism that was common among Middle Eastern Jews two thousand years ago. Many historians thought it was eradicated in AD 70 by the Romans, but unfortunately, it has been discovered that the disease mutated and eventually spread throughout Western civilization over many centuries. Eventually, it was brought to the Americas by the early settlers, and here it has flourished. It's believed that more than 75 percent of Americans today are exposed to this condition, and a very high percentage of our population suffers from this horrific condition without knowing.

Thankfully, there is a cure. Although it was a long, painful process for me to go through, I started on the remedy nearly twenty years ago. Since discovering it and experiencing the healing myself, I have devoted my life to identifying the cause of this blinding disease and to sharing its cure with those who have *ears to hear*. It is perplexing that the cure I discovered dates all the way back to the first century and needs no alteration. In its original form, it promises to heal the afflicted by bringing about eyes that can see as fully as they were designed, exceeding well beyond anyone's expectations.

As I said, the cure is not new, but since it is so closely connected to the cause, it often is overlooked. I found it while closely examining an ancient series of writings that are readily available to everyone afflicted. It is my hope that the book I have written will assist you or someone you love in diagnosing the symptoms early and overcoming the terribly contagious and rampant condition of Phariseeism that is permeating many parts of America, most commonly among Christian communities.

What exactly is Phariseeism?

Any person familiar with the life of Jesus and the persecution of his earliest followers, as written about in the New Testament scriptures, knows about this religious group, from whom I have named this condition. If you are unaware, the Pharisees were an ancient Jewish sect that emerged as the predominant religious leaders during the time of Jesus. They were very strict adherents to their religious beliefs, and they are the people mostly responsible for the crucifixion of Jesus and persecuting some of his earliest followers.

This once-popular sect of ancient Judaism devoutly sought to separate themselves culturally from all other people groups, as well as any Jew who did not practice or adhere strictly to the Mosaic laws and the authority of the temple. They had a great reverence not only for the written laws of the Torah, the first five books of the Bible, but also the oral traditions that were added over time. These pious men had great passion for the ways of God, but they made life extremely burdensome on their adherents. Though they were devout in their beliefs and practice, we read in the New Testament that both John the Baptist and Jesus of Nazareth called them out for their wickedness, hypocrisy, and abhorrent hearts. They loved their power and wealth and were willing to compromise their faith to maintain it.

They may have been culturally admired and upright to the religious standard, but Jesus saw them as blind to the ways of God and often pointed out that their hearts were far from him. This had nothing to do with their knowledge of the scriptures or the devotion with which they practiced their religion. Ultimately, their determination to keep a tradition- and performance-oriented focus led them into blindness of the truth, and they could not recognize the way or characteristics of God, even when it was right in front of them.

The inability to recognize God's true nature is the first sign of Phariseeism. The problem is that it is difficult to recognize our own inability to see something that is invisible in nature, especially if it is not "of this world," as Jesus said under trial about the kingdom of God. A Pharisee relies on human effort to be "set apart" from the world. Jesus and later the apostle Paul, a reformed Pharisee himself, spoke often against this human tendency, but eventually it worked its way right back into the beliefs and practices of the very people who claimed to be adherents to Jesus's and Paul's teachings.

Today, these people are most commonly called *Christians*.

The word Christian has many connotations, and depending on one's personal beliefs and experiences, they may be positive or negative. Regardless, we must acknowledge that it has become an extremely polarizing word today.

Many people are very proud to use the word *Christian*, just as I did for many years. It is hardly a coincidence that pride can be a *good Christian*'s greatest stumbling block. Ever since the enemy of

God used human pride to trip up man in the garden of Eden, God has warned us to guard against pride.

It was not just an issue for the Jews in the old covenant, but it continues to attack Christians in the same way it did for many years before Jesus. Many of the ancient prophets, such as Isaiah and Hosea, expressed God's distaste for what Israel's religious practices became, yet despite repeated correction, these devoutly religious people did not turn from their self-reliance or man-created traditions. Woefully, some of the very things from which Jesus came to free humankind have reemerged as the focal point for many Christians today, even as they wave the banner of Christ.

It is because of my personal background that I know this all too well.

As a child and adolescent, I was proudly an adherent to all things Christian, but I did not understand, fully or intimately, the true gospel of Jesus and its theme of the kingdom of God, and I carried that into my young adult years. I realize now that without a true understanding of Jesus and his kingdom, most Christians are simply practicing a modern form of Phariseeism. Only now it has a different doctrine, language, liturgy, and set of holidays than its Jewish predecessors.

God eventually made me aware of this, and that is why I am telling my story as a reformed and repentant evangelical Christian Pharisee—one who, although good at being a Christian, could not see the kingdom of God.

Part 2

More than ten years into my recovery from Phariseeism, I was still struggling with my spiritual sight. I had begun to thoughtfully question many of my experiences within the Christian culture to which I had been exposed in the Bible Belt of America because of what I read in scripture. I was wondering if or when I would experience the things that I was reading about in the New Testament, particularly those that pertained to my experience of God's power and my ability to understand his will and the active role of the Holy Spirit in my life.

I did not question my faith in God, the reliability of scripture, or Jesus's saving grace. I just questioned the fullness of my experiential knowledge of him and my engagement with the Spirit of God that was supposedly sent to dwell in me, guide me, and equip me with power to live an abundant life.

I never questioned God's sovereignty over all things or the role Jesus had played in my life to bring me into relationship with him. After all, I was taught from a very young age that when I prayed to receive Jesus as my Lord and Savior that he came to reside in my heart in the form of his Holy Spirit, and I talked to him often. Nevertheless, I knew something still was absent.

I was living what I thought was the good Christian life—I taught Bible studies, led church small groups, voted Republican (as I thought any good Christian was supposed to do), and even worked professionally in ministry. All the while, I felt lost, alone, and abandoned by the God I wanted to know fully and serve completely.

Even though I talked to God constantly, I questioned how to know and follow his will and trust the closeness of his presence in the circumstances of my life. I knew God loved me. I just wasn't sure if he *liked* me very much. He was not answering my prayers or showing up when I asked him to. He started to feel distant and impersonal, and I started to doubt how important I was to God and if he even truly cared for me.

Having grown up with faithful parents, attending Christian schools with Bible class every day, going to church on Sundays, and spending much time reading and studying scripture since I was in college, I had a very strong intellectual knowledge and foundation in Protestant Christian theology, albeit I struggled with my intimacy with God and desired so much more of him. It was here that I committed to work through this by diving more deeply into scripture than ever before. I began with the book of Acts because I wanted to know what changed when the first followers of Jesus received the Holy Spirit. I wanted to see what I was missing.

The book of Acts is a historical account of roughly the first three decades of the early followers and apostles of Jesus, written by the same individual who wrote the Gospel of Luke. Acts is an eyewitness recording of how the men and women of the first century who called themselves "followers of the Way" and "disciples of Jesus" (1) first received the Holy Spirit; (2) testified of what they personally witnessed of Jesus; (3) began the *ekklesia* (now commonly referred to as *church* and discussed later in this book); (4) spread the good news of the kingdom of God throughout the Middle East, North Africa, western Asia, and southern Europe to Jews and Gentiles; (5) imitated and multiplied the very work that Jesus modeled for them; and (6) established guiding principles consistent with Jesus's teaching for those living in the kingdom of God.

I knew the theme and most of the stories in Acts, but I needed God to specifically show me how he guides and directs those he calls into belief of his Son. I wanted to know how to do God's work and how to recognize his voice. So I dived in differently than I ever had before.

"Talk to me, God. I need *you* to reveal yourself to me," I often prayed as I opened my Bible.

I desired to be intellectually honest and was willing to abandon any preexisting belief I had if God would reveal it me. I had no agenda other than his. I committed to make reading my Bible— always with a pen in hand and a prayerful heart, trusting his Spirit to speak to me through scripture—a part-time job. I am grateful that he has answered my prayers, just as he promises to do when we ask, seek, and knock.

A principal foundation on which Jesus built his church and operates in his kingdom is God's revealing truth directly to man:

Jesus replied, "Blessed are you, Simon [son of John], because my Father in heaven has revealed this to you. You did not learn this from any human being … upon this [foundation stone I will be building my congregation], and all the powers of hell will not conquer it. And I will give you the keys to the Kingdom of Heaven." (Matthew 16:17–19 NLT, with translation edits)

As is true to his character, he has been faithful to deliver as promised in the process of giving me eyes to see and ears to hear ever since. I must admit, however, that he is much more patient in the process than I am, as it has not been instantaneous. It has been a journey that is still ongoing, and this book is only part of the journey that continues.

As I read Acts with new intent, I noticed that the disciples of Jesus and their brothers and sisters in Christ ministered and acted in an emboldened way that we rarely see today. They had a great conviction and certainty. Their lives bore eternal fruit that I desired to produce, and many around the Mediterranean rim, including Judea, Asia Minor, Greece, and much of the Roman Empire, came into amazing experiences of Jesus through the message of the gospel and the power of the Holy Spirit.

I was reminded of a verse that I had known for years: "Jesus Christ is the same yesterday and today and forever" (Hebrews 13:8). I was convinced that God would not deny me himself, but I also knew that the Jesus I wanted know fully was not going to be the same Jesus that I had known from my Christian experience up to that point.

I later realized that the verse prior to one above says, "Remember those who led you, who spoke the word of God to you; and considering the result of their conduct, imitate their faith." I began to wonder at what point the practice of imitation of those who had supposedly spoken the Word of God to me had as great a limitation of an intimate knowledge of Jesus as I did. They may have been *good Christians* too and likely more knowledgeable, but the more I read the scriptures of the Bible, the more I realized that I had never been led to the real life-giving Jesus.

What, then, was I imitating?

I was imitating the American church culture. I was led by

knowledgeable church pastors with seminary degrees, but nobody modeled to me how to humbly live out life in God's kingdom through their weaknesses, nor was I immersed in a body of believers who demonstrated dependency on the Holy Spirit and were committed to being disciples of Jesus.

I mostly knew the Jesus that was portrayed by a Western Christian worldview. I learned to be a Christian Pharisee to the expectations through the culture to which I was exposed and by people offering something other than Jesus and his gospel.

I was not taught in the way of Jesus as he lived and taught his disciples, nor did I understand the way the apostles expanded what they knew experientially. I was taught a religious model that has been evolving for nearly two thousand years from its origin.

I have sought to know what authentic discipleship of Jesus practically looks like in my life. In choosing to be an apprentice of Jesus by learning from those who trained under him, I have discovered that growth through apprenticing under Jesus far exceeds the knowledge found in academic Bible teaching.

Apprenticeship is a process that goes well beyond teaching theology and doctrine from scripture; rather, it is a process grounded in expectation of God's interactive work in our hearts. As I experientially learned through watching, listening, reading, praying, and practicing how to grow in my dependency of Jesus, I began to discover a different Jesus. Finding this type of Christ-follower to grow along with has not been easy. At times it has been a lonely endeavor.

Apprenticeship is dissimilar from academic learning, as it requires an *imitation* phase before ever implementing or innovating. The process of apprenticeship is all about learning on the job, learning from following and observing someone else's experience and application. It puts us in an environment for our own experiential learning, which is always better than just being taught good information. I have realized that this key phase of acquiring through imitating others who are imitating Jesus through active obedience often has been dismissed from modern-day Christianity. Obedience to Jesus has been replaced with intellectual knowledge about him.

We live in a society where information is so readily available that we can learn about almost anything. Head knowledge is not our problem, and it was not the problem of the Pharisees; experiential knowledge is our problem. We are so influenced by centuries of religious church practice and traditions that most Christians do not have an intimation of what it looks like to model their lives after Jesus or his followers.

Therefore, many—dare I say most—Christians in our civilized Western culture do not believe in what the disciples came to believe in, nor do they attempt to do what the disciples did. The disciples learned by watching Jesus depend on the power of the Holy Spirit, and once they received that power at Pentecost, nothing could stop them from carrying it out and multiplying the work of the Lord.

> Truly, truly, I say to you, he who believes in Me, the works that I do, he will do also; and greater works than these he will do; because I go to the Father. (John 14:12 NASB)

That is the life in Jesus that I want!

Apprenticeship of Jesus is not an original idea. It is a two-thousand-year-old concept that Jesus used and commanded as the methodology for all who would believe "until the end of the age" as the way to spread the good news of life in him and the kingdom of God. I have simply chosen to implement his way into my life. The impact has been more than life-changing; *it has been life-giving*. I invite you into my journey of redemption, from the trap of cultural Christianity into the way of Jesus.

A Good Christian

"You're *intimidating!*"

These words spoken by a coed in college forever changed the direction of my life. Those two words were used to eventually give me eyes to see and ears to hear far beyond what being a "good Christian" could ever offer. I know because I was good at being a Christian.

My grandma lived to be ninety-six, and she was a blessing to many people around her, as she always had a servant's heart. Even at the age of ninety-five, she believed her calling was to serve those in her assisted-living home who needed more help than she did. In addition to serving others so beautifully, she was thoughtful and always made people feel special on their birthdays. Every September I would receive a card in the mail with a little cash in it, and the note usually started with "To My Christian Grandson …"

Depending on your family of origin, that may not be that great of an accomplishment, but I know it meant something to her. She had the persistent belief that I was going to be a minister one day. As it turns out, she must have had the gift of prophecy in addition to service.

The "Christian" label from my grandmother was not unique; the marker was attached to me throughout my youth.

In the eighth grade, my private Christian school formed a student government association, and the faculty member who put it together asked me to be the school's first student-body chaplain. She thought I was a good Christian teenager.

In high school, I went to a different Christian school, where at the end of my freshman year, I was awarded the Timothy Award by the faculty, which was for the student who exemplified outstanding Christian character. (Good thing I didn't know they gave out such an award; I might have choked coming down the stretch!)

I was the poster boy of a "good Christian." I was the teenager whom mothers wanted their daughters to date and hopefully marry one day, which I eventually learned was the kiss of death with many girls during their rebellious years. (Fortunately, I didn't meet my wife until we were adults.) I was respectful, well-mannered, and clean-cut. I played three varsity sports; I made good grades; and I was class president on multiple occasions. I didn't drink, smoke, curse, or sleep with girls.

I did everything I thought I was supposed to do to be a good Christian.

My good behavior continued into college at Auburn University, and the "Christian" tag continued even as I joined one of the largest, most popular fraternities on campus. By my junior year, I already had worked one summer as a camp counselor at a Christian sports camp; I was on the student leadership team of a thriving campus ministry; and I was invited to be the first-ever college intern for a large national Christian sports ministry. By the time I was twenty-one, I still had never had a sip of alcohol, and I spent most of my time with other good Christians who shared commonalities in life, faith, and social behavior.

All of these were good things, but I would soon discover there was something very important missing.

This all leads up to a typical weekend night in Auburn, when several friends of mine were just hanging out as usual. I ended up in a conversation with a friend that forever changed my life. I don't know what we were talking about that set up the bomb my friend

Kerie was about to drop on me, but I will remember this line as long as I live:

"Josh, you're intimidating."

"What do you mean, I'm intimidating?" Unfortunately for my ego—but fortuitously for my heart—she was well prepared to back up her initial comment. She rattled off many things that exposed my prideful, self-reliant, performance-oriented approach to life; then came the two-by-four right between the eyes. "And for goodness sake, you're twenty-one and have never even had a drink!"

There was nothing wrong with being twenty-one and having abstained from alcohol, but Kerie had exposed something that was beneath my good behavior: pride. She had revealed to me a tremendous flaw, and I had absolutely no argument for anything she had said. My heart, though it had become callous from years of legalism, was penetrated, and I heard a message in my heart that felt as if it came straight from the Holy Spirit: "Josh, you're a Pharisee!"

If I was like a Pharisee, then I looked nothing like Jesus. I was the opposite of the one I thought I was emulating. I was the enemy of his work. I was more like Saul of Tarsus, who persecuted Jesus prior to his road-to-Damascus experience, than the converted Paul (Acts 9:15 NASB). This moment was my blinding light from heaven.

"Okay, let's go have a drink," I replied sheepishly. So Kerie and I went to a bar on College Street, where God strangely used my first drink to open me up to the transformational process that Jesus was ready to begin in my heart, mind, and soul. (Okay, technically I had only two sips, and I let Kerie have the rest because I didn't like whatever we ordered.) It was the transformational work that only Jesus can do. This process continues today.

I know many people have testimonies where they quit drinking when they became Christians, but have you ever heard about a faith-based journey that grew from a sip of alcohol? I like to tell people, "I started drinking when I found Jesus!" (For the record, Jesus was accused by the Pharisees of being a drunkard in Matthew 11:19 and Luke 7:34. I'm just sayin', perhaps you shouldn't judge!)

Of course, this book has absolutely nothing to do with encouraging you to compromise any personal decisions or guardrails you have established for your life to avoid sin. Rather, it has everything to do with the state of your heart and mind. The legalism, pride, selfishness, and performance-based mentality that many Christians carry often prevent us from walking intimately and vulnerably with Jesus and each other.

John the Baptist said it best: "He must increase, but I must decrease" (John 3:30 NASB). I had to learn to get lower. I had to get off my throne and learn to sit at the feet of Jesus in utter dependence of him.

I had much need for growth, despite being a good Christian.

Desiring the Way of Jesus

Performance-based faith is burdensome. It is a heavy load that we were never meant to haul around through life in Jesus. For many years, I thought God's two favorite words were *no* and *don't*. The reality is that the commandments of the new covenant are *dos*, not *thou shalt nots*.

He says, "My yoke is easy to bear, and the burden I give you is light" (Matthew 11:30 NLT). The good news of Jesus is not a religious doctrine. A strong faith in him is not about being good at sin management—real self-control is a fruit of the Spirit that is produced when we remain in Jesus and when the new life he has created replaces our old nature. Christian culture often presents a problem in its expectations of performance.

When we are born again into our new spiritual lives, we do not perceive it as okay to be babies who have to learn to crawl and walk before we can run and play in the kingdom of God. Our culture often casts an unfair expectation of maturity for an early believer, and this is where the trap of self-reliant performance is established and often never overcome.

Like many others, I followed a religion that I thought was of

God because I adhered to the expectations of faithful Christians. I thought I had a good grasp of the scriptures and Christian theology, but like the Pharisees and other religious zealots in the time of Jesus, I tried to earn God's favor through my own abilities and by checking off all the boxes. I just happened to be proficient at it. Thankfully, God used the conversation with Kerie, who was willing to challenge me, as a catalyst to eventually help me realize that the type of faith I had was not what Jesus modeled or taught, nor was it what his disciples and apostles emphasized as they spread the good news of Jesus and his kingdom.

I am so grateful that God desired so much more for me than what I thought I knew from my Christian experiences; he wanted to capture my heart, not just my behavior. Even though I thought Jesus was my foundation, it turned out that he was not—I was! I drew upon my own strength, a strength he had given me for a bigger purpose one day than just to be a good Christian by society's standards.

I thought I was good at sin management until I realized that my pride was a great sin I could not manage. I had to admit that my faith was more reliant on my performance than on God's power. I had only trusted in Jesus to take care of my sins (even though I didn't think I needed as much grace as most people) so that I could have assurance of going to heaven when I die. I can even remember telling a close friend that the lyrics of "Amazing Grace" didn't really connect with me. But now I want it to be played by a bagpiper at my funeral as an archer shoots a flaming arrow onto my gasoline-soaked raft as is floats out to sea! I never saw myself as a wretch who needed saving.

I certainly was not blind to the truth. After all, I was a "good Christian."

As it turned out, even though I had prayed to accept Jesus into my heart as a young child, I had never truly repented. The word *repent* does not just mean to ask for forgiveness of sin; it is to turn and go in a different direction. Jesus revealed this direction to the world, and it was a sharp contrast to religion that humans can manage.

When Jesus began his ministry, Mark writes that he was "preaching the gospel of God, and saying, 'The time is fulfilled, and the kingdom of God is at hand: repent and believe in the gospel'" (Mark 1:15 NASB). At age six, I became a Christian because I believed Jesus died for my sins, but it was not until I was twenty-one that I turned the direction of my life and began to trust in the true gospel of God, which is Jesus and life in and through him.

My character did not change immediately. Soon after college, some friends nicknamed me "Oge" because it was the word *ego* backwards. Obviously, I was still a great work in progress.

It was not until a few years later, when circumstances in life were not working out as well as I had planned, that God was able to do significant work on my heart, but the conversation with my friend Kerie truly changed the direction of my life forever. I eventually would accept that all my good behavior would not necessarily be rewarded in this life, but that he had much more in store for me than I could imagine. He was going to reveal to me the good news of Jesus and the kingdom of God to give me an abundant life in it.

> The kingdom of heaven is like a treasure hidden in the field, which a man found and hid again; and from joy over it he goes and sells all that he has and buys that field. Again, the kingdom of heaven is like a merchant seeking fine pearls, and upon finding one pearl of great value, he went and sold all that he had and bought it. (Matthew 13:44–46 NASB)

I wanted whatever it was that Jesus said was worth giving up everything to have. So through much introspection, many honest questions, hundreds of hours of prayerful reading of scripture, and thoughtful investigation, I became convinced that my life's pursuit is to grow into the likeness of the greatest teacher who ever lived—Jesus.

My prayer for you is that as you read through the journey on which God has taken me, it may help you examine your own heart and experience as a Christian. I pray that God will use elements of this book to equip you with tools, truths, and insight to apply the appropriate personal responses to the Holy Spirit's work in your life, as he has mine. My hope is that you will accept his offer to apprentice under Jesus, just as the authors of the New Testament did, so that he may teach you to fish for men and become a thirtyfold, sixtyfold, hundredfold producer of fruit in his kingdom. His desire is that you will come to know him in such a way that he will flow out of you rivers of living water. Christianity cannot do this; only Jesus can.

FISHING WITHOUT BAIT

And Jesus said to them, "Follow Me, and I will make you become fishers of men."

—Mark 1:17

"You cannot give away what you do not possess," the president of the ministry of which I am on staff reminds us often. Unfortunately, many Christians try to share a gospel and a "belief" that they have not truly discovered for themselves. The by-product of this is a Christian culture throughout the world that claims to be in Christ and Christ in them but that does not know the person of Jesus or represent his true character. Many are trying to do great works for God on their own power but fail to recognize, "The work of God is this: to believe in the one he has sent" (John 6:29 NIV).

I know this to be true because I did this for most of my Christian life. Many Christians have knowledge, as I had, of some form of Christian doctrine that they were taught and can offer a reasonable defense of their theology. While many claim to have a faith in Jesus and an indwelling of his Holy Spirit, it is much harder to find Christians with an overflowing abundance of the fruit and power of him. However, Jesus said, "You will know them by their fruits" (Matthew 7:16 NASB), and Paul wrote, "For the kingdom of God does not consist in [puffed up] words but in power" (1 Corinthians 4:20 NASB).

Most of us have never truly experienced the power of God, but we are trying to live the Christian life and even evangelize in his name.

Again, *you cannot give away what you do not possess* (unless you are a politician in Washington, DC).

Jesus understood this principle and dedicated his ministry to giving away the kingdom of God to his disciples and to all he ministered. He threw all his chips into one simple strategy: Teach the twelve how to fish for men.

My nine-year-old son, Caleb, loves to fish. For the last four years, he has asked almost exclusively for "fishing stuff" for birthdays and Christmas. Even when he is not out fishing in the ponds in our neighborhood, he often goes through his tackle boxes to get set up to catch his next big fish. He likes to show me his newest lures, sometimes ones he's made himself, and he tells me what type of fish will like which one or what color works best, depending on the time of day, season, and clarity of the water. He knows more about fishing than I do because he is consumed with it. He asks tons of questions to anyone he meets when fishing (or anywhere else, if someone is wearing clothes or a hat that resembles a fisherman).

"Caught anything?" he loves to ask others who are fishing. If the answer is yes, he follows up with, "What bait are you using?" He, of course, wants to know what will work for him to catch fish. He wants to know what the fish are attracted to and what they are not. Then, he tries to negotiate a trade with his brother, cousins, Pappy, or any other victim who crosses his path who has fishing equipment. He offers everything he has that doesn't work in exchange for whatever might give him a better chance of catching fish. Maybe we could learn a little bit from him.

> "I'm telling you, once and for all, that unless you
> return to square one and start over like children,
> you're not even going to get a look at the kingdom,
> let alone get in." (Matthew 18:3 MSG)

I love Caleb's enthusiasm for fishing. He can tell you every lure he used to catch all of his biggest fish. (Like a true fisherman, the fish get bigger and bigger the more he tells the stories.)

When I come home from work, he often says, "Dad, I caught a bass today."

"Awesome, buddy! What did you catch it on?"

He can always tell me what he was using. Poignantly, he has never said it was on a hook without a lure or bait.

For Caleb's birthday party a couple of years ago, we had a fishing party at one of the ponds in our neighborhood that has a nice dock and play area. We invited all his classmates from school and brought all our fishing equipment for the kids to use. For some reason, though, most of the kids (other than Caleb)—those who managed to miss the tree limbs overhanging the dock and get their lines into the water—did not catch any fish. Frequently I would ask one of the children to reel in the line to check the bait; often, there was nothing on the end but a shiny little hook.

It was obvious why Caleb caught the most fish that day. He was fishing with bait in the water.

Most evangelical Christians I know, including myself for years, are fishing without bait on the hook when it comes to being fishers for men. That is, of course, if they even take Jesus's invitation to become a fisher of men seriously. I know that many Christians see their faith as a personal matter and believe the role of growing the body of Christ is for pastors, clergy, professional ministers, missionaries, and Sunday school or Bible study leaders, but Jesus did not invite us to be Christians. Jesus's invitation was to be disciples, which simply means students or learners of him. The great commission was more than a great suggestion, and it was not just for his twelve disciples.

Jesus launched a multiplying ministry that was to be engaged by all who would believe in their message. He prayed at the Last Supper, "I do not ask on behalf of these alone, but for those also who believe in Me through their word; that they may all be one; even as You, Father, are in Me and I in You, that they also may be in Us, so that the world may believe that You sent Me" (John 17:20–21 NASB). Jesus prayed this for you and me, that we would reveal him to the world around us. The problem, even with most evangelicals who desire to bring others into faith in Jesus, is that they are fishing without anything on the hook, or what is cast into the water is the completely wrong type of bait. It is not attractive or alluring to the fish.

Learning to Bait Our Hooks

It became obvious to me that people were not lining up to know more about my faith because I was simply a good Christian by cultural standards. If anything, I might have been a repellant. This is not because people don't find good people appealing. We all want them as neighbors, bosses, employees, coworkers, and in-laws. (My experience is that this does not necessarily apply to the contractor who shows up at your house with a Christian fish on the side of his truck or van.) If we are to attract people to the gospel, which is the person of Jesus, they must be attracted to his flowing out of us. Time and time again in the four Gospels, we read about how the crowds were astonished and amazed with the work and teachings of Jesus; after Pentecost, the same was true for his disciples and apostles.

> Everyone spoke well of him and was amazed by the gracious words that came from his lips. "How can this be?" they asked. "Isn't this Joseph's son?" (Luke 4:22 NLT)

> When Jesus had finished saying these things, the crowds were amazed at his teaching, for he taught with real authority—quite unlike their teachers of religious law. (Matthew 7:28–29 NLT)

When the Sabbath came, He began to teach in the synagogue; and the many listeners were astonished, saying, "Where did this man get these things, and what is this wisdom given to Him, and such miracles as these performed by His hands?" (Mark 6:2 NASB)

Day by day continuing with one mind in the temple, and breaking bread from house to house, they were taking their meals together with gladness and sincerity of heart, praising God and having favor with all the people. And the Lord was adding to their number day by day those who were being saved. (Acts 2:46–47 NASB)

Time and time again, onlookers recognized something about the character of Jesus that was glorious, but I did not have in me the same glory and grace that grew the body of Christ throughout the Roman Empire, Africa, and Asia before it was religionized. I especially realized that I was lacking what the apostles had when life threw me curveballs because I only knew how to rely on myself during difficult times. I prayed for God to show up and help, but I did not know how to lean on him as Paul did. "You also became imitators of us and of the Lord, having received the word in much tribulation with the joy of the Holy Spirit, so that you became an example to all the believers in Macedonia and in Achaia" (1 Thessalonians 1:6–7 NASB).

Paul, Silas, and Timothy found joy from God in the midst of their trials, and they encouraged those who imitated them because they knew they were imitating Christ himself.

This is what I was missing. I was sure that I had the Holy Spirit living inside me, based on what the teachings of my youth had assured me, but I was not bearing multiplying fruit. I was not overflowing living water.

Though I could quote many Bible passages, argue with apologetics, explain the Four Spiritual Laws to salvation (a common evangelical practice made popular by Bill Bright of Campus Crusade for Christ), and had a very strong grasp of Christian theology, I did not have anything on my hook that lured fish into God's kingdom.

Could it have been that even though I had asked Jesus into my heart as a child that I did not know the true gospel of Jesus?

I was blind, just like the many people Jesus referenced who could not see the kingdom of God. Christian culture and churches today are full of blind men and women trying to guide others into the kingdom, which they do not see themselves. Too often, Christianity just offers an intellectual belief system that is blind to the power of God. All along, I thought I wanted people to know Jesus as I did, but since I still did not know him experientially or intimately, it turns out that I really wanted them to know what I believed.

As Carl Medearis writes in *Speaking of Jesus: The Art of Not-Evangelism*, "We do not really know the gospel. It's part of a multifaceted tapestry of other things. We have misplaced the gospel, perhaps become blind to it. It has become hidden in sermons, churches, self-help books, and apologetic philosophies."

What was I still missing? I did have the Holy Spirit, didn't I?

I had prayed the Sinners Prayer when I was a young, had been baptized in my church, and had grown in my knowledge of scripture (I even signed a pledge for abstinence in a middle-school youth group and kept it until I got married), but I was still thirsty, and living water did not flow out of me.

Medearis adds, "The distance between people and Jesus isn't doctrinal. It isn't political or social or even theological. It's a matter of personal contact. Jesus collided with two fishermen, and their lives were changed. In fact, the world was changed. That's because Jesus is, in Himself, the gospel. Once He makes contact, our hearts struggle within us, and we, like Peter and Andrew, have to choose to follow or not."

Living Water

If you've ever been fishing below a dam or where a river flows into the ocean, you know the fish are attracted to where the fresh flowing water is. My water, on the other hand, was stagnant, and I didn't understand why. I was like the church in Laodicea that was told in Revelation, "Since you are like lukewarm water, neither hot nor cold, I will spit you out of my mouth!" (Revelation 3:16 NLT).

There is a good reason why Starbucks has a hot menu and a cold-drink menu but no lukewarm menu; it's simply not palatable. My heart had become stagnant, so of course it did not attract others to drink from it.

By the time I was a young adult, I already had become like the prideful, spiritually dead church in Laodicea. I offered no refreshment, despite my Christian accolades. God wants us to be more like the water sources of the nearby cities of Colossae and Hierapolis, instead of the stagnant water in Laodicea.

Colossae was known for its cold water, sourced from the mountains, that brought great refreshment, and Hierapolis had the hot springs of Pamukkale that provided soothing, therapeutic benefits for those who came to bathe in its waters. Laodicea, on the other hand, despite its great wealth and prosperity, did not have fresh water. In fact, its water was putrid and stagnant; it was undrinkable.

Like the city's water supply, this church was useless to the service of the Lord, as their worldly prosperity and spiritual pride got in the way of producing his fruits. Nobody wanted what they had to offer, and nobody outside of my Christian circles wanted what I had to offer either.

Despite my knowledge of the Bible and obedience to the rules of my religion, I was blind to the ways of God. My heart was developing a spiritual callus that, on its current program, would only keep thickening. I needed to change course, but I thought I was on the right one. I was *living* the Christian life well, but I was not *walking* in the way of Jesus, nor was I obeying his commands.

Jesus said in the presence of his disciples and the religious leaders, "A blind man cannot guide a blind man, can he? Will they not both fall into a pit? A pupil is not above his teacher; but everyone, after he has been fully trained, will be like his teacher" (Luke 6:39–40 NASB). I was a student of Christianity but not of Jesus. Jesus taught his students to fish for men. He modeled something so attractive. He modeled how to depend on the Holy Spirit to do the will of his Father and to love the world through the fruits of the Spirit. Jesus revealed the character of God as it could be lived out of a man. He showed us how to love others well.

> "For I gave you an example that you also should do as I did to you." (John 13:15 NASB)

As you read on, you will discover the process of how God baits our hooks with attractive bait that is of him. This is not a recipe for a quick fix to successful evangelism. God is too personal for that. Rather, this is my journey of learning to leave the way of the world behind, even cultural Christianity, to follow Jesus as a lifelong disciple of him. I finally chose to abandon my way and began to be a multiplier in his way. I now serve and minister to others by clinging to Jesus, and I am still learning to become fully dependent on him to partner with him in his work.

He has invited you to do the same. He does not call us to practice Christianity or to ascend to a sound biblical doctrine. He calls us to listen to his teachings, obey his commandments, and follow him all the way to our glorious completion. He says, "Anyone who listens to my teaching and follows it is wise, like a person who builds a house on solid rock" (Matthew 7:24 NLT).

I was not a student of Jesus in my youth; rather, I was a student of a religion using his name that had evolved over two thousand years. I was becoming like Saul of Tarsus, a well-intended religious zealot, persecuting the ministry of the Lord. I needed to get to know the real Jesus if I ever was to have an effective ministry of the good news of Jesus that would expand the kingdom of God.

By God's grace, I now know Jesus and progressively see and experience more of his kingdom, and I did not find it through liturgical practices, self-discipline, or any corporate production of Christian worship commonly available in our culture. Rather, I found it in time spent alone with him, reading and praying through scripture and beginning to put it into action. In my brokenness and repentance and, ultimately, through submission and surrender to him and his will, I began to see the kingdom of heaven.

Much like the apostle Paul noted to the Philippians—"I don't mean to say that I have already achieved these things or that I have already reached perfection. But I press on to possess that perfection for which Christ Jesus first possessed me" (Philippians 3:13 NLT)—I too am not there, but I will complete the task that God has put before me. I will follow him so that I may become like my teacher. Through him, I am going to be a thirtyfold, sixtyfold, hundredfold producer in his kingdom.

Worthy of Being Imitated

> "Brethren, join in following my example, and observe those who walk according to the pattern you have in us." (Philippians 3:17 NASB)

Allow me the following analogy: If I weighed 250 pounds on my relatively slight five-foot-ten frame, nobody would be waiting in line to get on my diet and exercise program at first glance. However, if I showed someone a picture of me weighing a hundred pounds more just a couple of years prior, you might think I'm on a program worth following. That is the discipleship process of which I am testifying. I still have progress to make to be fully mature and complete, but I am on a glorious path that is worth imitating because

I am following the example and teachings of Jesus and imitating those who imitated him.

After the day of Pentecost, when the disciples became filled with the Holy Spirit, they knew only one thing to do—continue living as Jesus had taught and modeled. It should not surprise us that "each day the Lord added to their fellowship those who were being saved."

If we want fish to bite, maybe we should return to the manner and to the things Jesus taught and stop focusing on our religious practices that have little contextual foundation in the New Testament. As Dallas Willard points out in *The Great Omission: Reclaiming Jesus's Essential Teachings on Discipleship*, "The word 'DISCIPLE' occurs 269 times in the New Testament. 'Christian' is found three times. The New Testament is a [collection of books] about disciples, by disciples, and for disciples of Jesus."

Willard later states, "For at least several decades the churches of the Western world have not made discipleship a condition of being a Christian. One is not required to be, or to intend to be, a disciple in order to become a Christian, and one may remain a Christian without any signs of progress toward discipleship. So far as the visible Christian institutions of our day are concerned, *discipleship clearly is optional.*" Then he adds, "Most problems in contemporary churches can be explained by the fact that members have never decided to follow Christ."

God has some work to do in our hearts to bait our hooks with something appetizing. This is crucial to living in harmony with the work of Jesus. We all must realize that we need training in the way of his kingdom. We must become disciples of Jesus. The problem, as I see it, is that the enemy is using Christianity to deceive us, just as he did Judaism with the culture in the time of Jesus.

The enemy wants us to believe that if we have sound doctrine, are consistent in our religious practices, and manage good moral behavior that we are right where God wants us. We are being good Christians.

The problem with this belief system is that it innately encourages us to hide our flaws and showcase our strengths (much like Facebook and Instagram). We end up living artificial lives, trying to get others to bite on our lifeless, fake lure, when what they really want and need is live bait.

THE DOUGHNUT HOLE

During the disciples' three-year apprenticeship of Jesus, they often heard him call out the most religious men of their time. On one occasion, Jesus referred to these publicly esteemed men of religious law as "whitewashed tombs, which on the outside appear beautiful, but inside they are full of dead men's bones and all uncleanness" (Matthew 23:27 NASB).

Jesus saw these pillars of the community differently than their public perception; he could see the state of their hearts, and they were dead on the inside. I have a feeling Jesus would say the same thing about many Christians today; at least, I know he did to me years ago, when he revealed to me that I resembled a Pharisee more than I did Jesus. I was not aware that my heart was building up walls of spiritual plaque and becoming unhealthy.

Jesus lived roughly fifteen hundred years after God gave the Israelites their Law. By this time, it had been turned into a religion with various sects that added to it their own man-made traditions, teachings, and beliefs. Though the Law was meant to eventually be replaced by something better, the new covenant through his Son, the nation of Israel had strayed far from their obedience to what God had commanded of them. They had lost their way not only in worship and practice but in heart.

God's children were no longer a light to the world.

Fatefully, Christians have had nearly two thousand years to drift from the way of Jesus. Over time, well-meaning Christians have religionized and added to the even better covenant that God gave to the world through Jesus. Knowing man's tendencies, we really should not be that surprised or defensive about the suggestion that Christianity has migrated from its starting place of discipleship of Jesus.

Christianity, as it has become, is mostly a religious construct of man, supported by the parts of scripture that affirm its practices and teaching. Today, it is hard to find in Christian circles what Jesus brought into the world. Sound Christian doctrines can very well explain salvation through Jesus alone, but they often miss in explaining the ongoing experience we have with the gospel.

The enemy deceives us to think we can create a better model, just as he did Israel, by placing the emphasis on creed, doctrine, and man-made rules and practices that are manageable by human effort, instead of compelling us to address our drifting, decaying hearts.

Christianity has replaced the authority of Jesus and the living and active leadership role of the Holy Spirit with biblical doctrine. As well, the body of Christ has shifted from *ekklesia*—the Greek word later substituted by the word *church*, which has several possible meanings, but none translates to a building or institution—with the modern church model. We have returned, in many ways, to the very temple model from which Jesus came to free us.

We have done this in many ways, but most notably it is in the context of church. You will be hard-pressed to find much contextual biblical evidence to support the manner at which most churches operate in today's Western cultures; ironically, they usually teach from the very scriptures that do not give evidence for many common practices.

It is also difficult to find "discipleship" programs that imitate the methodology of Jesus. Most discipleship programs are classes full of instruction and intense Bible study. Recently, I had someone tell me he signed up for a discipleship program at his church, and when I asked him to tell me more about it, he said the group was on a plan to read through the Bible in a year. I think reading through the Bible in a year is wonderful, but what does that have to do with growing as a disciple of Jesus? Others have told me about groups they are in where they do exhaustive verse-by-verse studies of the books of the Bible.

Maybe I missed it, but I cannot recall a time in the four Gospels where Jesus called the twelve around him and said, "All right, guys, today we're going to begin our verse-by-verse examination of the scrolls of Isaiah to see what he really meant."

Don't get me wrong; I cherish my Bible reading and study time, but Christians have replaced *doing* what it says with *knowing* what it says. We emphasize knowledge of scripture and praise in-depth teaching, but knowledge and good teaching rarely change our routines, actions, or life directions.

Jesus said, "Everyone who hears these words of Mine and does not act on them, will be like a foolish man who built his house on the sand" (Matthew 7:26 NASB). God is much less concerned with how much you know than he is with what you do with what you know.

There is great purpose in learning the scriptures, as Jesus displayed by quoting them often, though it always had a practical application to life in his kingdom. He never got into contests with the Pharisees to see who could quote the most verses. The purpose of scripture is not for us to have head knowledge of it; rather, it is to guide us in action—to follow Jesus.

Jesus constantly gave his disciples tasks to do to put their budding faith into action. He understood that the disciples' greatest opportunities for growth would come from experiential learning. We must be in action and relationship to grow as well. We cannot live out all the "one another" commands of the New Testament if we just sit in a pew or classroom attempting to feed our minds with knowledge.

It is so important to understand what happened for us when Jesus died for our sins. He took care of our need to work on self. We no longer need to work on getting right with God. By putting our faith and trust in Jesus, we are made right with God forever. Jesus's death and resurrection fulfilled all the covenants that God made with his children from Abraham through David, and it ushered in a new and better covenant, just as Jeremiah prophesied:

> "Behold, days are coming" declares the Lord, "when I will make a new covenant with the house of Israel and with the house of Judah, not like the covenant which I made with their fathers ... I will put My law within them and on their heart I will write it; and I will be their God, and they shall be My people ... for I will forgive their iniquity, and their sin I will remember no more." (Jeremiah 31:31-34 NASB)

The author of Hebrews quotes this passage and writes, "When He said 'A new covenant,' He has made the first obsolete. But whatever is becoming obsolete and growing old is ready to disappear. For when the priesthood is changed, of necessity there takes place a change of law also" (Hebrews 8:13; 7:12 NASB).

This helps us understand why Jesus could offer one simple law for living in the new covenant: "A new commandment I give to you, that you love one another, even as I have loved you, that you also will love one another" (John 13:34 NASB).

Love requires action; it is not a feeling or a thought.

Discipleship of Jesus is the process of learning how to love others well. That is our purpose. We are to be lovers of God and lovers of others. "By this all men will know that you are my disciples, if you have love for one another" (John 13:35 NASB). Sadly, this is no longer what Christians are known for in today's culture. We are better known for what we are against than what we are for.

It is evident that cultural Christianity is not healing the hearts of its adherents.

Consuming Church

How would you describe your church to someone of another culture who had never been a Christian or knew nothing of Christianity?

Maybe you are one of the few with a different experience than I have had over the years, but I would describe it as a big building where my family and many others, who hardly know each other, go on Sundays to sit in many rows of seats to worship God together—that can vary greatly, depending on denomination—and then learn from one of the leaders of the organization through a prepared lesson or teaching that we call a sermon. We call these big weekly events, which people refer to as "going to church," a worship service. Most big churches have multiple worship services on Sundays, but each one is pretty much the same, so you pick the time that works best for you.

Granted, some churches still do something called Sunday school in addition to the worship service, where you sit in a smaller room with fewer people to learn a little more from another teacher. Other churches, like mine, have incorporated smaller group environments called community groups, which meet in a home, but these environments are often established to learn more about how to be a good Christian as well.

I then would need to explain how a church is organized: There is a professional church staff of clergy or pastors and some operational employees who work there for a living, and then there are volunteers who help with some of the activities and environment, but for the most part, the church staff plans and orchestrates everything in which we get to participate. It all costs money, so it is up to the members to give part of their incomes to cover all the operating costs.

At the end of the day, that is all most of us ever really know or experience of church. We walk into a building and spend an hour or so participating in whatever our church staff has arranged for us to experience during our time there, and then we leave and go about the rest of our lives.

Other than the staff and volunteers who put everything on for the congregation, the majority of Christians are only expected to show up and consume what they have produced. There is no active role for the congregation, other than—depending on your denomination—reciting a creed, responding in unison to scripted lines, singing along with the worship leaders, and then sitting quietly while you listen to the pastor's sermon.

I am sorry if this description is offensive or sounds cynical. I am a member of a large church in Atlanta and support it both financially and by serving in some of its environments. However, it is because of my love for the body of Christ that I am addressing the way church culture has evolved, from its beautiful foundation of expected active participation and inclusion of the congregation at gatherings to sitting back and absorbing what has been put together for consumption.

To some extent, church in America has become a rehearsed and perfectly orchestrated performance, where most services could go off without a glitch. Frankly, nobody would ever know if the Holy Spirit was even involved. We trust that he is guiding our pastors and leaders, but at the end of the day, we do not depend on the Holy Spirit to lead our time together, and when we show up, we certainly do not expect to have any contribution to the service, other than being a silent body in a seat, receiving that which was prepared for us in advance by the staff.

This is an abiblical practice. This does not mean that what most churches are doing is wrong; it is just that what we call church in America is not the model we find in the Bible or know was practiced in the first century.

Paul instructed the church in Corinth, when gathering, to look like this:

Well, my brothers and sisters, let's summarize. When you meet together, one will sing, another will teach, another will tell some special revelation God has given, one will speak in tongues, and another will interpret what is said. But everything that is done must strengthen all of you. (1 Corinthians 14:26 NLT)

So when the first-century churches came together, the congregation was expected and expecting to participate with their own spiritual gifts to edify one another. This was never meant to be changed, and it disappoints me that most church experiences in America are more about the quality of music and teaching than interaction—far from the scriptural precedent. When we gather to worship, we all should all so dependent on the Holy Spirit to lead us and work through us, just as Paul expressed above, that there is no way we could have a perfectly predetermined program.

I know what you are probably thinking. We have hundreds or even thousands who attend our church every Sunday; this would be chaos. You're right! I am not suggesting that churches stop doing worship services. Many of us have grown very fond of them. I am proposing, however, that churches take a hard look at what they are doing to facilitate relational growth, discipleship of the congregation, and involvement that requires faithful action and dependence on the Holy Spirit. This is how we grow. We do not grow from the teaching alone.

Paul wrote to the church in Ephesus, "And He gave some as apostles, and some as prophets, and some as evangelists, and some as pastors and teachers, for the equipping of the saints for the work of service, to the building up of the body of Christ" (Ephesians 4:11 NASB).

The congregation is the saints, and the pastors and teachers are supposed to be there to use their gifts to equip us to do the work of service and to be the church. It was never intended for our pastors and church staff to feel the responsibility of spoon-feeding the congregation every Sunday.

The evolution of church and the abandonment of the practices established in the first century has created a culture of passive participation. This passivity that happens in corporate church gatherings carries over to our individual lives. Often, we feel as if our Christian faith is experienced only as consumers and lived out only through personal expression and prearranged experiences. Thus, we are a culture of hybrids, people who have one foot firmly planted in the world, determined to gain in every possible way from it, and one foot crossing the line into a version of Christianity, which accommodates our other loves. This hybrid model allows people of faith to pick and choose certain parts of their religious experiences to emphasize and chiefly ignore the real themes of the teaching of Jesus and the documented lives of his earliest followers.

I like to call this *Jesus sprinkles.* (My kids think every food is better with sprinkles on top, especially ice cream, cupcakes, and doughnuts.) Most Christian organizations, ministers, and individuals are simply sprinkling the parts of the Bible and teachings of Jesus that satisfy their appetites. Today's churches and seminaries have become the manufacturing facilities for millions of whitewashed tombs, only these are not made of granite or marble like you see in a cemetery; rather, these are the hearts, minds, and souls of men and women practicing an abiblical religion called Christianity. We are like a box of doughnuts that looks appetizing but offers nothing but fat, sugar, and gluten, with no real nourishment. Sadly, the more you consume, the more harmful it potentially becomes because your knowledge is built up, but your heart is ignored.

Despite what you hear, read, and likely have been taught, Jesus did not start a religion, nor did he create church as we know it. Jesus established a practice and culture of life-changing apprenticeship, rooted in the denial of self and the love of others. Just before ascending into heaven, Jesus left his disciples with their commissioning: "Go therefore and make disciples of all nations, [immersing] them in the [character] of the Father and the Son and the Holy Spirit, teaching them to observe all that I commanded you; and lo, I am with you always, even to the end of the age."

The age has not ended; therefore, this is our commissioning as well. Jesus has not instructed us to make Christians or practice a religion in his name. Rather, he has commanded us to be disciples and make disciples by teaching what Jesus taught and modeled. In this endeavor, he promises to always be with us.

The "In" Club

Twice recorded in Matthew's Gospel, Jesus quoted the prophet Hosea to the religious leaders, "I want you to show mercy, not offer sacrifices." He was insistent that God wants our hearts, not our religious practices. The earliest followers of Jesus did not call themselves Christians; they referred to themselves as disciples or followers of the Way, as Jesus claimed to be "the way." He replaced the temple model of the Old Testament with a better way of intimacy with God. Jesus changed the entire nature of man's ability to have relationship with God. He did not establish a better way to do religion; he threw religion out the door. Christianity is a religious model that many choose. Some claim they are Christians by birth or because of infant baptism, and regardless of how sound theology and teaching is, we must recognize that many of the things we are exposed to in Christianity is of human construct.

We do not have biblical evidence that suggests that the early disciples or apostles ever referred to themselves or their practices as being Christian. There are only three uses of the word Christian in the Bible. It could be argued that each use actually carries a negative connotation. We should not be offended by the word, but it does not adequately describe what Jesus established or his disciples multiplied. Because the followers of Jesus proclaimed him to be the *christos*, "the anointed one," outsiders who did not understand their faith started calling them Christians for following this so-called "Christ." There is absolutely nothing wrong with the term, as it was a name that others attached to the disciples who followed and proclaimed Jesus. Nevertheless, it was not how they self-identified.

It is not important to me what you call yourself; rather, I care more about the process that takes place in your heart. A lifelong student never stops learning and growing, but since one becomes a "Christian" in an instant, the term can easily allow one to become complacent in his or her growth. My concern for personally using the word is that it describes where one already is, not where one is heading.

When people claim to be Christians, they usually are not implying that they are on spiritual journeys as they follow Jesus. Instead, it usually describes where they already have arrived, as if they are in an exclusive club. The word *Christian* does not imply constant growth, and it is not centered around a process of the heart that Jesus came to nourish and fill with himself.

Sadly, the connotations of the word Christian in most parts of the world today do not reflect the character or person of Jesus. Christians are often characterized as judgmental, hypocritical, narrow-minded, and homophobic. To many people, it defines one's social and political views.

Jesus and his earliest followers were labeled many things, but these were not among them. They went out of their way to love and serve the world around them. It was these characteristics that made them so attractive. They taught within to abstain from immoral behavior, but they compassionately pursued people who lived the way they did not.

Paul emphasized this:

> I wrote to you in my letter not to associate with immoral people; I did not at all mean with the immoral people of this world, or with the covetous and swindlers, or with idolaters, for then you would

have to go out of the world. But actually, I wrote to you not to associate with any so-called brother if he is an immoral person, or covetous or idolater, or a reviler, or a drunkard, or swindler—not even such a one. For what have I to do with judging outsiders? Do you not judge those who are within the church? But those who are outside, God judges. REMOVE THE WICKED FROM AMONG YOURSELVES. (1 Corinthians 5:10–13 NASB)

We are to hold accountable those within the body of Christ, but it is not our role to judge those who never committed to follow Jesus. The problem with many Christians today is that they judge those outside our faith and hold very little accountability to those within. This is opposite of what see in the accounts of Jesus. He challenged those who thought they were already "in" and showed compassion and mercy on the corrupt tax collectors, prostitutes, adulterers, and disenfranchised.

According to Jesus's explanation of the well-known parable (often referred to as the Parable of the Seed and Soils, found first in Matthew 13:1–17) to his disciples, there are many who will never receive or understand the word of the kingdom. However, there are those who accept and receive the gospel but, due to not establishing deep roots in Jesus, turn away when they face affliction or persecution. Then there are those who do establish growth in their faith, but as their faith grows, so also does the worry of the world and the deceitfulness of wealth. These things eventually choke out the kingdom of God.

This is the group to whom this book is predominantly written. In our culture, we can be good Christians who check all the religious boxes and grow in our knowledge but never know the power of Jesus on the inside. Jesus said, "It is not those who are healthy who need a physician, but those who are sick; I did not come to call the righteous, but sinners" (Mark 2:17 NASB). Many Christians do not see their ongoing need for Jesus, as I didn't for many years. They think they are "in" because they claim Jesus to be their Savior, but they never grow in their experiential knowledge. They grow in theological knowledge but never really know Jesus.

> "Not everyone who says to me, 'Lord, Lord,' will enter the kingdom of heaven, but only the one who does the will of my Father who is in heaven. Many will say to me on that day, 'Lord, Lord, did we not prophesy in your name and in your name drive out demons and in your name perform many miracles?' Then I will tell them plainly, 'I never knew you. Away from me, you evildoers!'" (Matthew 7:21–23 NASB)

American Christians are often encouraged to pursue everything this world can offer, as long as it is not immoral, while at the same time trying to pursue the eternal promises of God. In God's grace, anything is possible, but Jesus brought forth a different teaching as to how we enter the kingdom of God. He taught that we cannot serve both God and the things of this world. Jesus said that his kingdom has a *narrow road and very few will enter it.* My concern is for the people who lived like I did in my past, separating my faith from my life's pursuits. As a Christian, I claimed the promises of Jesus and declared him as Lord and Savior, but I had not turned to Jesus to change the direction of my life. Many Christians choose the parts of the Bible and teachings of Jesus that fit comfortably into their plans. We fully accept John 3:16 but give little attention to John 3:3, which says *we must be born again.* (I am not saying that you don't claim to be born again.)

By picking and choosing what works for us, many feel as if they can obligate God to give them eternal life in heaven after death because they believe in Jesus, but they would rather have the things of this world than that which he came to give.

Many Christians never choose to enter the kingdom of God, as taught by Jesus, to experience the abundant life that has been made available to us now.

The simplest explanation for the kingdom of God is that it is *now* and *not yet*. I have great concern for the direction of anyone who does not pursue the now but wants to obligate God to the not-yet part. This is the have-our-cake-and-eat-it-too mentality of many Christians. I do not know what judgment is to be had for this approach, but it certainly is not what Jesus taught, and we should not put our hope in human-derived doctrines that replace the thematic teachings of Jesus. This often-adopted attitude of the Christian faith puts the obligation on God's grace to make up for the direction of our lives by replacing *the way* Jesus revealed with our own personal belief systems and our focus on performance-based living.

How We Got Here

Performance-based living was common in Israel two thousand years ago, and it has become the grading system of Christianity in the Westernized world today—a breeding ground for internal decay, just like Jesus pointed out in the Pharisees. As mentioned in the preface, this eventually leads to a spiritual blindness that prevents us from seeing the kingdom of God. I call this place where we hide all our pride and spiritual decay our doughnut hole. (Ironically, these are the very things many churches proudly serve in Sunday school or the fellowship hall with coffee.)

For years, followers of Jesus attracted people into community with the Lord because onlookers desired what they had. These imitators of Jesus became known for their love and compassion for others, just as the Lord modeled. However, they knew they could not do the work of the Lord on their own power; they were dependent on the Holy Spirit for everything they did. They wanted to give away to others the same healing power that they had experienced in their own lives. "For the kingdom of God does not consist in words but in power." People were attracted to the God-given power of the believers. They witnessed people living completely changed lives—lives changed inside out, from the heart into action.

For nearly three hundred years after the resurrection of Jesus, it was illegal in the Roman Empire to worship Jesus. Believers met peacefully and quietly in homes; there were no church buildings or 501(c)(3) organizations. Instead, there were men and women who were part of local assemblies called *ekklesias*, committed to participate in and bring forth the kingdom of God, about which Jesus spent his entire ministry living out and teaching. There was no social benefit for being a part of this movement, and it certainly was not viewed as a recipe for a better life—a more peaceful and joyful life, yes, but not more comfortable.

Despite the probability of persecution, this kingdom movement spread throughout the entire Roman Empire and beyond within three decades of Jesus's resurrection. Historians of their time who documented the so-called "Christians" marveled at the courage and joy of these early martyrs.

How could the body of Christ survive under such intense persecution? The amazing fact is that it not only survived, but it thrived! The body of Christ was strengthened by persecution. It was when the persecutions stopped after nearly three hundred years of oppression that we start to see contamination and abandonment of what was working so well. Within the safety and prosperity of the United States, it is no wonder that we find Christianity so different from its roots.

It has been written throughout history that "the blood of the martyrs is the seed of the Church." Tertullian, a man who lived during the days of the early persecution, said it this way: "Go on, rack, torture, grind us to powder: our numbers increase in proportion as ye mow us down. The blood of Christians is their harvest seed." (http://www.middletownbiblechurch.org/missions/miss7.htm)

History has proved this statement to be true. Many enemies of the Christian church have been converted in faith simply by watching and witnessing the bravery of true believers as they faced death. Their purpose was to continue the mission of Jesus and realize the vision he cast for their lives—to be a light to a dark world. They did not set out to create and practice a new and better religion. They were following the way, the truth, and the life that only was found in following Jesus, and they wanted everyone else to have the same freedom that they had found in Christ.

It was not until Constantine and Licinius issued the Edict of Milan in 313 that Christian worship was decriminalized (Wikipedia, "Constantine the Great and Christianity"). Under rule of Diocletian, in the ten years leading up to this, the Roman Empire had attempted to wipe out Christianity completely. Despite this, it continued to grow. By 380, Christianity had become the official religion of the empire.

In sixty-seven years, it went from being illegal to worship Jesus to the entire Roman Empire enforcing a Christian doctrine. From the start of the fourth century to the end, Christians went from being a persecuted group to, at times, a persecuting people. They went from being known for their love and compassion to being known for their doctrine. They went from turning death into life, peril into hope, blindness into sight, and many other characteristics of healing into formality, structure, and religion. This newly found power that Christians gained forever changed the landscape and culture of what we call Christianity.

The reason for this brief history lesson is to point out how the process of mission drift began to invade Christianity. What was once a mission to heal the substance of our doughnut holes eventually became the process of making beautiful doughnuts with icing and sprinkles on top—why we find throughout American Christian culture so many religious people who are nothing more than whitewashed tombs.

The Doughnut Hole, Finally

Almost two thousand years ago, God began revealing and enacting the kingdom of God, which was available to all people through Jesus, along with the promise of his presence in our lives. It came through the good news of freedom, healing, eternal life, joy, and, ultimately, victory over sin and death. Over the years, I have interacted with many professing Christians who are angry, bitter, controlling, fearful, and prideful but claim Jesus as Savior for their sins. I cannot judge their hearts, but I do not observe the fruits of the Spirit. Many others will clean up their acts to put on a show for others, but when you get to know them, you can see that there is little peace on the inside.

Jesus said that he came to fill all things with himself, so why, then, are so many professing Christians as empty as I was? Jesus wants us to have rivers of living water flowing out of us; instead, fear, anger, doubt, greed, anxiety, loneliness, lust, pride, depression, and despair are stirring in us. Discipleship of Jesus is the process of replacing these characteristics of the flesh with the fruits of the spirit by allowing the Lord to heal and renew the real us, thus turn our eternal character into love, joy, peace, patience, kindness, goodness, gentleness, faithfulness, and self-control.

We cannot do it on our own initiative. If we could, we already would have done so by now. (Must be why I have never successfully kept a New Year's resolution into the month of February either.) Jesus understood the human tendency, and that is why he said, "This is the only work God wants from you: Believe in the one he has sent" (John 6:29 NLT). He knows that individuals want to do impressive things on their own. Unfortunately, because we have abandoned discipleship in Christian culture, many of us don't have authentic modeling of what it looks like to be dependent on God. We do not have churches full of people who believe God has given them the keys to his kingdom—binding all that is bound in heaven and experiencing all that is loosed in heaven, as Christ declared when he launched his ekklesia in Matthew 16:19.

Instead of authentic, lifelong apprentices of Jesus guiding us into the healing power of Christ, today we most often settle for being led by the most devoutly religious, Bible-knowledgeable individuals, who attempt to guide us into a good Christian life, all the while hiding the things in their hearts that still are dominated by pride and lack of faith. We have seminary graduates teaching us doctrines that often include theories of why we don't experience God's power today in the same way they did in the first century, never realizing that unbelief is the source that keeps them from realizing it for themselves.

One of the great problems of today's Christian culture is that it has settled for not experiencing all that God wants to give us. So many of our ministry leaders are well-presented on the outside but struggling on the inside, with no safe place to turn. It is rare to find transparency from the pulpit; consequently, we experience very little authenticity in the Christian community, and church does not feel like a safe place.

Our doubts and fears are often fueled by Sunday sermons that remind us of our flaws. We are unaware of the struggles going on internally in others' lives, particularly our leadership. This forces Christians to put on a show in order to hide the real us from everyone else. We sweep the dirt under the rug and throw all the junk in the ugly room, shut and lock the door, and allow no one to enter, including Jesus.

Maybe I should have said *especially Jesus*, the one who is standing at the door, knocking, with a mop, broom, and sanitation gloves.

Despite perfect church attendance and the bonus points we hope we get for being in a Bible study or small group, many Christians develop a thicker callus around their hearts as head knowledge outgrows personal experience of Jesus. Thus, we seek affirmation from those in our church who likely are just better than we are at acting like good Christians.

We serve and worship alongside each other. We take communion together, and our statements of faith align with similar doctrines, yet we bear little to no eternal fruit and don't know why. We are nowhere close to thirtyfold, sixtyfold, hundredfold producers in the kingdom of God—that is, if we even understand what the kingdom of God is! (I will address the kingdom of God in greater detail later in this book.)

The pressure is now on. Am I not reading my Bible enough? Was my tithing supposed to be before taxes? Am I being punished for a sin in my life that I'm not managing well? If I go on a mission trip, will that get me back in the plus-column or at least get me on a spiritual high, like the last night at youth camp where I got to throw my sin into a big bonfire?

What is that? Where does that come from?

It certainly wasn't Jesus. He made peace with us by going to the cross and dying for our sins. He took care of every barrier that gets in the way of our being in right-standing with God. Romans 8:1 says, "There is now no condemnation for those in Christ Jesus." Therefore, there is no need for us to keep trying to work out what God already took care of. God wants us to move beyond the cross and into the kingdom in which he reigns. He wants us to grow and become mature in our new creation. Simply assenting to a certain religious viewpoint intellectually or getting good at going through the motions does not help us find favor with God.

When Jesus referenced Hosea's prophecy—"For I delight in loyalty rather than sacrifice, and in the knowledge of God rather than burnt offerings" (Hosea 6:6 NASB)—he was communicating God's desire for us to know him in our hearts. Our New Testament translations usually quote Jesus as saying *mercy* or *compassion* instead of *loyalty*. God wants the entirety of our hearts, not just our religious acts to be done in his name, and that is why he sent Jesus to manifest him to us.

In addition to Hosea, another Old Testament prophet told Israel something very similar. In Isaiah's first chapter, the Lord says to

Israel, "What are your multiplied sacrifices to Me? I have had enough of burnt offerings of rams and the fat of fed cattle; and I take no pleasure in the blood of bulls, lambs or goats. Bring your worthless offerings no longer … they have become a burden to Me."

Despite their continual warnings, Israel became more and more religious and farther from God. They turned their laws and prophecies into a religion we now call Judaism. For clarification, when I use the word *religion*, I am referring to something that, regardless if it is attached to truth, has eventually become about human effort, practice, and beliefs that are established to earn the favor of God. Religion is built when humans replace walking faithfully in dependence of God with the ability to perform for God. The Jews turned dependence and loyalty to God into pride and dependency of self; I also see this in the evolution of Christianity.

I am convinced that many of the same things for which Jesus called out the Pharisees and Sadducees, he would be calling out Christian leaders today.

It is not hard to fool your fellow man with your religion, but you cannot fool God. He knows our hearts. The very religious Jews in the time of Jesus looked good on the outside, but Jesus said they were empty on the inside. I was a good Christian on the outside, but I too was empty on the inside. As we try to find a balance to life that works and is manageable, we often continue with a void that does not get filled, and we all know it is there.

This void is the doughnut hole of cultural Christianity. It is the "real us" that we find when we dive beneath the surface, if we never have allowed Jesus to truly reign in our hearts and turn our minds in a heavenly direction. It looks like this:

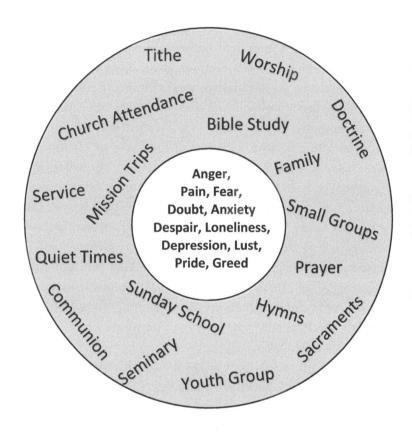

When we understand how the kingdom of God works, we realize that Jesus did not come to earth so that we could just go to heaven when we die; rather, Jesus came to open up heaven to earth.

With our cooperation, Jesus will fill all things with himself—and that includes our hearts. He came to restore our relationship with heaven. As Jesus launched into his public ministry, he preached a very consistent message: "Repent, for the Kingdom of Heaven is at hand" (Matthew 4:17 NASB). Note: Only Matthew uses the phrase "Kingdom of Heaven"; the other three Gospel writers use the phrase "Kingdom of God."

The word *repent* means to turn in a different direction. It does not mean to confess or feel sorry for your sins and continue in the same direction. God wants us to turn the entire direction of our earthly lives, which once led to death and destruction. He wants a complete paradigm shift in our thinking so that we may see the way of his kingdom and live as Christ.

Many Christians have never turned around to go the way of Jesus. Instead, the common practice is to make our lives more Christian through behavior modification. We might change some of our activities and behavior, but the direction of our lives is no more heavenly than before. We simply just added Jesus sprinkles to our doughnuts and still have our doughnut hole with all doubts and unbelief of what Jesus already has accomplished on our behalf. We are yet to be filled with Jesus and the joy and peace that comes with his presence.

One of the greatest mysteries to me is how little the kingdom of God is taught or discussed in most Christian circles, despite its being the central theme of everything Jesus taught. Many Christians to whom I talk assume, as I did for many years, that the kingdom of God that Jesus spoke about so often is the place we all hope to go when we die. This explains why many live just as I was—trying to manage life well and trying to meet the expectations that our church culture has of a good Christian but not seeking complete transformation of the mind. This common theme among Christians has no contextual backing from scripture, as it is inconsistent with the predominant theme of everything Jesus taught:

> Jesus went into Galilee, where he preached God's Good News. "The time promised by God has come at last!" he announced. "The Kingdom of God is near! Repent of your sins and believe the Good News." (Mark 1:14–15)

The Greek word used here for "is near"—and used several other times by Jesus to refer to the kingdom of heaven—in the original manuscripts is *eggiken*. Some Bible translations even less appropriately say "is coming soon," but since *eggiken* is a past-present

Greek word, Jesus was telling us that the kingdom "has come" and is "upon us" and "in us!"

This is supported by numerous other claims of Jesus, and the good news of the kingdom of God was characterized by healing, freedom, and the defeat of sin, pain, and darkness, among other glorious attributes. It would not be fulfilled and accomplished for his followers until his death on the cross, but if this is why Jesus came, then why are most Christians not yet claiming their victory over sin? Unfortunately, many in the church love to remind us of our sin and fail to lead us into kingdom living now.

I may still give in to some of the temptations of sin and the part of my flesh that still desires the things of this world, but I am a child of God.

I was a sinner, saved by grace ... but now I am a co-heir of Jesus, crucified and made dead to sin with him, declared righteous, and told to forget the past and finish the race for which I have been called in Christ.

I have a new identity in Christ, and you do too.

If you had beaten cancer and were given the all-clear from your doctor, would you continue to live as if you had cancer? Would you continue to go back for more radiation and chemo, just in case, if your doctor did not recommend it? No, you would get as far away from those treatments as possible, as long as you had a clean bill of health.

As well, if you were once homeless and had found a way out of your extreme poverty and eventually became wealthy, just as Benjamin Franklin did, would you continue to live on the streets? No way! You would claim your new life of victory.

So why do you say that your sins have been forgiven because of Jesus's death and resurrection, but you continue to wallow around in them?

Though you may have areas where you still need to gain more insights into life in the kingdom of God, the real issue is that nobody has ever led you into the light of living in Jesus. It's possible you haven't been apprenticed in the way of Jesus. You might have been taught much about Jesus and the religion that eventually formed in his name, but quite possibly no one ever modeled life in Jesus to you in a manner that you could follow.

Most of us are Timothys without an apostle Paul in our lives. Without someone modeling Christ's transformation and life in his kingdom, we often are left with nothing more than the Christian religion and our own interpretation of how to check its boxes.

I know this because the award I won in my freshman year of high school for Outstanding Christian Character was called the Timothy Award. I knew how to be a good Christian, but I did not rely on the power of the Holy Spirit to live as Christ. I behaved well on my own willpower, with a fear of punishment from God if I didn't. I was trying to earn God's favor, rather than receiving his grace that is full of power.

We all need someone to remind us, "It may be true that you struggle with your anger, or doubt, or fear, or lust, but that is no longer who you are." The truth is that you are none of those things. Therefore, *what is true about you is no longer the truth about you*— because the truth came to live inside you, and his name is Jesus. He knows no sin; in his glory, he is set apart from it. Because of that, he makes a pure place in our hearts to dwell, grow, and live out through us. He has placed a part of the kingdom of heaven inside all believers, sanctifying us in the likeness of Christ.

This is portrayed in several of Jesus's parables, most notably the one of the seed and soils mentioned earlier. God has planted the seed of the kingdom in you. Have you watered it and given it room to grow?

Christians claim to have the seed planted in them, but the maturing process that Jesus desires stalls way too early because many do not properly tend the soil. We do not allow God to be our gardener.

Remember that the seed that fell among the thorns grew but eventually was choked out. This soil and seed is the American

Christian culture. Many have received God's Word as their faith, but they do not let it take deep root or allow it to be choked out by the ways of the world.

Religion can be a worldly trap, as it cannot create fruit-producing soil. Only Jesus can produce fruit. He doesn't want us to attempt to be appealing doughnuts; rather, he wants to tend to and nourish the soil of our hearts—the doughnut hole.

Statistically, an increasing percentage of Americans are rejecting the Christian faith more than we have ever seen in previous generations. However, 1.3 billion people in the world claim to be Christians. The problem is not that we need to make more Christians; it is that the world is full of people claiming Christianity who have never invited Jesus to work on their doughnut hole.

Many minds have chosen to believe in Jesus for access to God and heaven when they die. For various reasons, however, they have not let their spiritual roots grow deep in the person of Jesus, or they have allowed the lure and distractions of this world to suffocate and defeat their hearts. It is for these reasons that the civilized Western world is full of professing Christians and devoid of the power of the Holy Spirit—a power that is fully capable of cleaning up the mess of our doughnut holes.

If you look deep enough into a spiritual mirror, past your religion and its practices, do you still see something ugly? Do you still find yourself working on the sin Christ already defeated on the cross? This book was written to invite you into a life that leaves all that stuff at the foot of the cross and so you will begin to pursue a heavenly direction now. That is the real purpose of discipleship of Jesus. Jesus's students learn what it looks like to nurture good soil, the final type that the seed fell into in the parable. It represents those who truly hear and understand God's Word and produce an eternal harvest that is thirty, sixty, or even a hundred times as much as was planted.

This is what Jesus meant for us when he said, "I tell you the truth, anyone who believes in me will do the same works I have done, and even greater works, because I am going to be with the Father.

You can ask for anything in my name, and I will do it, so that the Son can bring glory to the Father. Yes, ask me for anything in my name, and I will do it!" (John 14:12–14 NASB).

We all want to live a life of significance. Could there be a greater life than that of a multiplier of Jesus? I do not believe there is. Come let us grow together. Let's partner with the Holy Spirit so that he may finish what he started. I cannot promise you that it won't hurt (or as doctors like to say, "You might feel a little pressure").

You may have to let him do some spiritual tilling of rocky ground or break out the weed whacker and hedge clippers for the overgrowth in your life that's focused on the kingdom of this world. That is why Jesus came, died, and rose from the dead—so that we may share in his glorious inheritance, now and forever!

STARTING OVER

In the Christian culture in which I grew up, most claimed to be born again. This comes from the recorded conversation Jesus had with a Pharisee named Nicodemus in the third chapter of the Gospel of John.

So I must ask: Exactly what part of *born again* is so hard for us to understand ... besides the being "born again" part? This phrase is frustrating to so many people, especially non-Christians. Why? Because they know too many people who claim to be born-again Christians who act no different than they did prior to being born again.

This very thought is something I wrestled with for many years. I had asked Jesus to come into my heart when I was six years old, which means I had been born again. However, I can hardly remember anything before I became a Christian, and I certainly don't remember experiencing any kind of significant change in my life. In most ways, I was just beginning to develop, so how could I be born again when I had yet to mature in my own flesh? What part of me was the new creation, and what part of me was the continuation of the old?

I was told throughout most of my life that the Holy Spirit was my conscience, but my friends who were not believers in Jesus had a conscience also. I recognize that even atheists have a conscience, even if they believe that their thoughts were prewired and that they have no choice but to act upon their programmed thoughts. So what was different about my conscience?

It is quite possible that I just carried around more guilt than most people. I certainly did not know freedom.

As I matured as a child and an adolescent, I made many good choices. I was not perfect, of course, but I was a good Christian by cultural standards. To my dismay, there was something that still troubled me. How could I be a new creation in Jesus if I couldn't tell the difference between the new me and the old me?

Was it possible that I had never repented or turned from my original path to the way of Jesus? Was I nothing more than a moralist who claimed Christ? I simply took the religion and faith of Christianity with me down my own path and tried to make the two work together.

It was like I was driving the car down the highway of life and had put God in the back seat. All I did was periodically check the rearview mirror to make sure he was still there. I occasionally asked him for directions, but I never let him drive or determine where we were going.

If I had let him drive, I would have risked his turning us in a different direction. He might have had the audacity to take control and go where he knew was best. I couldn't take the risk of that leading to missionary work in Africa, so I kept firm control of the wheel and justified to myself that I was a good Christian because I managed most of the dos and don'ts of my faith. I was good at obeying my religion, even though I was not very good at obeying what Jesus taught. I claimed to be born again because I had said a special prayer when I was a child, but I had gone through most of my Christian life without ever turning in the direction that Jesus modeled for me.

Jesus said to Nicodemus in the third chapter of John, "Unless one is born again he cannot see the kingdom of God." I hope we are all clear that when Jesus referred to the kingdom of God, he was not just talking about where we go when we die. (In a later chapter of this book, we will dive deeper into our understanding of this Gospel, but for now, I want us to stay in the moment of Jesus's conversation with Nicodemus.) He said we cannot see the kingdom of God unless we are *born again*. I don't know about you, but if Jesus said this, then I am certain that I want to be born again.

Note: If you are still trying to decide about the authority of Jesus's teaching in your life, let me tell you how I view it; maybe that will help. When someone predicts that he will die and rise from the dead three days later—and then he pulls it off—I am inclined to pay attention to everything else he had to say.

Because of my theology, I considered myself to be a born-again Christian, but was I? *Born again* can mean only one thing—a new life has begun. It means we must start over. It is supposed to be a new life or at least a complete renovation of the old. It is a tearing down of the old and the start of a new. I do not recall ever tearing anything down.

I've done a few residential real estate projects over the years, where I've both built a new house and renovated an old house, and though both can look beautiful at the end, the renovated house always carries some liability when you leave the original foundation. If nothing else, the wiring and plumbing must be new.

We must be rewired as a new creation—and I still needed to be rewired!

At one house project, we tore everything out of the old house except the original foundation from the 1940s, and we added off the back and then built a new two-story house on top of it. All seemed to be going well until some heavy rains came, and water came into the old crawl space. We ended up spending a lot more time and money to fix the old foundation than we would have spent if we had just torn it all out and started with a new foundation from the very beginning.

What is your foundation in Jesus?

Statistics show that over 90 percent of professing Christians accept their faith in Jesus before adulthood. This means that most of us, while developing our worldviews and being educated on how to operate in it, also try to develop our Christian faith. This idea of being born again while still in the developing years of adolescence can be very confusing; therefore, we tend to try to raise good Christian children from the start. Only a small percentage of Christians have testimonies of truly being born again, despite many claiming to be born again.

Many of us talk about growing up in the church, where we eventually accepted our parents' faith at Vacation Bible School, church camp, or a high school or college ministry that suggested we needed Jesus in our lives. We wanted to be forgiven of our sins so that we could be assured of going to heaven when we died.

In the evangelical denominations, many of us were led with a simple prayer to invite Jesus into our hearts. Maybe you intellectually decided to get on board with what your parents, pastor, or priest taught you through most of your life. A relatively small percentage of professing Christians live as adults who head down a path they later recognize leads to destruction and then choose to turn in the way of Jesus. Therefore, most of us were trying to figure out how to live a life as good Christians when various situations entered our lives.

Sadly, many Christians are led by pastors, teachers, parents, and friends who never really understood the process of being born again in their own lives. Because of this, "born again" has become nothing more than a biblical phrase we have borrowed culturally to believe in a faith that requires us to live by a certain moral code and obligates God to receive us in heaven when we die.

If we are to be born again, Jesus says we must repent. Christians often use the word in a way that implies we must ask for forgiveness and keep moving until we need to repent for that sin again. Remember, the word *repent* means to think completely differently about something or to turn in a completely different direction and go another way. It does not mean to keep going in the same direction but to do it in a better way. Unfortunately, this is the gospel that many of us were taught without realizing it.

We need the gospel that Jesus taught!

The message of repentance was taught not just to the people living the most immoral or secular lives; it also was preached by both John the Baptist and Jesus to the most devoutly religious people of their time. These religious people were told to turn from their evil ways. For some, their sin was their pride, self-reliance, and hypocrisy; it wasn't necessarily sexual immorality, drunkenness, debauchery, or other visible acts. This is where I found myself in my Christian faith as an adult. I was managing my outward performance and morality well, but I had never repented and followed Jesus. I had never died to self.

"Repent of your sins and turn to God, for the Kingdom of Heaven has come. (Matthew 3:2)" This was John the Baptist's message as he prepared the way for the Lord's coming. He said to the religious leaders of his time, "Prove by the way you live that you have repented of your sins and turned to God." Jesus continued to challenge these devoutly religious people to change their hearts and live it out, despite their attempts to live in perfect compliance to the Law.

Have you ever turned from your ways?

I'm not talking about stopping an immoral behavior through your own efforts because of your faith. The Pharisees did that very well, but they were still told to repent. I'm talking about something different. Your testimony may include that you stopped doing certain bad things when you became a Christian. That's great—those behaviors have no place in the kingdom of God—but did you ever relearn how to live your life? How to live in dependency of Jesus?

Did you ever learn to live and love like Jesus?

Here's a bit of checklist for you:

✓ When your wealthy friend comes home and tells you all about his incredible, luxurious vacation that cost more than you have in the bank, are you jealous?

- ✓ When your business competitor goes out of business, do you celebrate her failures?
- ✓ When you hear of a terrorist bombing, do you hope the Muslim extremist was killed?
- ✓ When your best friend's perfect teenager is trying to decide which Ivy League college scholarship to accept and asks you to pray for his wisdom, do you pray genuinely with him?
- ✓ When you are an Auburn fan and Alabama loses a football game, are you sympathetic to your Alabama coworkers who complain about the bad calls their team got on Monday? (Okay, maybe I went a little far with that one; I'm sure Jesus gets a lot of pleasure out of seeing an Alabama fan humbled!)

Jesus claimed that he did nothing for his own agenda, but he only did what the Father in heaven willed. Jesus did not believe his life belonged to him and neither does a well-trained disciple of his. Jesus said to his students, "A pupil is not above his teacher; but everyone, after [they have] been fully trained, will be like his teacher" (Luke 6:40).

To be born again, we must give our lives to becoming like our teacher—to become [perfected] and [completed], just as God is (Matthew 5:48). Let me remind you what the apostle Paul wrote in his letter to the believers in Philippi:

> Not that I have already obtained it or have already become perfect, but I press on so that I may lay hold of that for which also I was laid hold of by Christ Jesus. Brethren, I do not regard myself as having laid hold of it yet; but one thing I do: forgetting what lies behind and reaching forward to what lies ahead. Brethren, join in following my example, and observe those who walk according to the pattern you have in us. (Philippians 3:12-13, 17 NASB)

Unfortunately, most of us have never seen this modeled. We have been taught Christian doctrine and theology and been asked to live exemplary lives as Christians, but most of us have never been led toward completion, which is nothing more and nothing less than wholeness in Jesus.

Instead, most of us say something like, "I am a sinner and always will be."

Who told you that? It certainly wasn't Jesus or the ones he taught.

I believe it was men and women who have never truly been born again, despite what they claim. Those who teach this are the individuals who have never died to sin but who are trying to do life well and are failing constantly at it. Those who truly die to self, however, consider their lives of no value apart from Jesus, in his process of perfection.

This perfect completion to which God has called us is not achieved by human effort; rather, it is by the Holy Spirit's work that we submit every area of our lives to him to mature us. "Are you so foolish? Having begun by the Spirit, are you now being perfected by the flesh?" Paul wrote to the Galatians. Christians often try to be good on their own efforts; true disciples of Jesus are perfected by his Spirit as they die to self and live as Christ. There is a significant void in those of us who merely claim to be Christians and those who have chosen to follow Jesus to the end.

Without thoughtful examination of what Jesus taught, Christians too often accept the good things we have heard and overlook that which would challenge the other areas of our lives. Jesus, however, taught something that many do not want to hear. He taught us to die to self, take up our own crosses, and follow him. He taught us to kill our natural desires.

This means we must learn to die—or at least choose to lose.

CHOOSE TO LOSE

One reason I'm asking you to stop calling me Christian is because Christianity in the West has allowed us to continue with our own personal agendas for years, as long as we accept and agree with a certain doctrine and moral behavior. This is not what Jesus taught. Jesus taught his followers, by his own example, to give up their own selfish desires for the sake of putting others first and to give up the things of this world for the sake of eternal treasure. You cannot move forward in the process of discipleship without surrendering your life to Jesus.

Surrender is the first step and only path to growth and maturity in him. We all should find ourselves in a little bit of turmoil and chaos at this point. After all, most of us have been managing life quite well. We have found an element of order and believe we can manage it from here. This should be the starting place of surrender, not control. This is where we must face our fears. We must learn to die to self. We must learn the value of losing our own identities so that we may identify with Christ.

This is where we learn the value of our future glory above our present selves. We must trust that Christ is actively at work in all things on behalf of the kingdom of God, but we must *learn to lose* if we want to gain in it.

"If you cling to your life, you will lose it; but if you give up your life for me, you will find it," Jesus says to his disciples in Matthew 10:39, and he continues throughout his ministry. He teaches us to give up our lives: "And everyone who has given up houses or brothers or sisters or father or mother or children or property, for my sake, will receive a hundred times as much in return and will inherit eternal life. But many who are the greatest now will be least important then, and those who seem least important now will be the greatest then" (Matthew 19:30).

I don't know about you, but I didn't become a Christian when I was a child to lose my life. I became a Christian so that I could save it for eternity. I didn't follow Jesus so that I could learn to fish for men. I followed what I thought were the teachings of Jesus so that I could earn good favor with God and live a blessed life—but that is not the way of Jesus. He taught us to love others relentlessly by taking up our own crosses and dying to self. Dying to self is a process. We must learn to die, and, in turn, this is where we learn to truly love and live in his joy.

The best definition I have ever heard for love is *to fight for the best possible outcome in the lives of others.* Jesus modeled this for us. He revealed to the world what it was like to be God as a man. He was a relentless lover of others. He said, "I did not come to be served, but to serve, and to give my life as a ransom for many." For those of us who needed a simpler understanding of the greatest commandment—to love God with all your heart, soul, mind, and strength and to love your neighbor as yourself—he later simplified his entire teaching with this: "A new command I give to you, that you love one another; as I have loved you, you are also to love one another."

The obstacle in our lives that gets in the way of our doing this well is ourselves. Our selfish ambitions, greed, pride, jealousy, and so many other human tendencies get in the way. These are the issues in our doughnut holes (from the previous chapter) that Jesus came to redeem. These characteristics of the flesh are to be removed from our lives, and we must work in cooperation with the Holy Spirit to kill them. This is not only a part of discipleship; it is the core. This is what God desires for each one of us. Remember, "The disciple that is well trained, will become like his teacher." He wants us to become like him. Jesus taught his disciples to do this well before he revealed to them who he was—the Son of the living God—and before he gave them the power of the Holy Spirit.

A common misunderstanding in the Christian faith is that we are still sinners after being cleansed by Jesus. It is true that our flesh remains with us, but on the cross, Jesus took away the power of sin and darkness in our lives and cut away our sinful flesh from our new spirits. It is because of this amazing grace that we are made new creations. Paul wrote in Colossians:

> When you came to Christ, you were "circumcised," but not by a physical procedure. Christ performed a spiritual circumcision – the cutting away of your sinful nature. For you were buried with Christ when you were baptized. And with him you were raised to new life because you trusted the mighty power of God, who raised Christ from the dead.
>
> Since you have been raised to new life with Christ, set your sights on the realities of heaven, where Christ sits in the place of honor at God's right hand. Think about the things of heaven, not the things of earth. For you died to this life, and your real life is hidden with Christ in God.
>
> You used to do these [evil] things when your life was still part of this world. But now is the time to get rid of [them]. Put on your new nature, and be renewed as you learn to know you Creator and become like him. (Colossians 2:11-12; 3:1-2; 3:7-8, 10 NLT)

If this was not the case, Paul would not have written it. Paul also acknowledged that it was a process and that he had not yet reached perfection, as discussed previously.

I don't mean to say that I have already achieved these things or that I have already reached perfection. But I press on to possess that perfection for which Christ Jesus first possessed me. No, dear brothers and sisters, I have not [yet] achieved it, but I focus on this one thing: Forgetting the past and looking forward to what lies ahead. I press on to reach the end of the race and received the prize for which God, through Christ Jesus, is calling us. Let all who are spiritually mature agree on these things. (Philippians 3:12–15a NLT)

We have been called to this mind-set, and we are told in this same letter to the Philippians that we "must have the same attitude that Christ Jesus had," an attitude of loving one another by not being selfish or trying to impress others. He says, "Be humble, thinking of others as better than yourselves. Don't look out only for your own interests, but take an interest in others, too." This attitude can be accomplished only when we submit to Christ and look to him to give us his ability to love others above self.

Jesus told his disciples, "Your love for one another will prove to the world that you are my disciples" (John 13:35 NLT). He gave them this everlasting and overarching command right after washing their feet. "And since I, your Lord and Teacher, have washed your feet, you ought to wash each other's feet. I have given you an example to follow. Do as I have done to you."

If we do not fully realize what Jesus has done for us, then we cannot die to self. If you have fallen prey to the cultural version of Christianity that lends itself to Phariseeism, as I did, you likely have focused only on the development of yourself. This is where your faith becomes a self-righteous pursuit. Christianity has become very narcissistic and far from what Jesus modeled.

The discipleship of Jesus is not about the one being discipled; rather, it is about being the means to Jesus's end goal. Following

Jesus is not about each of us individually; rather, it is about him and his mission. We, individually, are not the end goal. Therefore, our religious faith cannot merely be academic in nature, an intellectual agreement in doctrine, and/or good sin management in daily life; rather, it must be the denial of self and the complete pursuit of Jesus's purpose.

Others Focused

For a long time, I thought I was the purpose of my faith. You have likely experienced the same thing. You listen to good teaching, read and study on your own, and you feel like you are responsible for your own spiritual growth. Granted, there are aspects of our faith that we have to work out in our minds and live out in our own behavior, but did you know that there are fifty-nine "one another" commands in the New Testament?

Fifty-nine! That is a lot of commands from the Lord that cannot be obeyed individually by working on yourself.

When Jesus called his disciples, he called them into a communal relationship. He didn't come just so you could invite him into your heart. He came to form a community of followers who would carry his mission to the ends of the earth. His mission was the kingdom of God, and his means to pull it off is his ekklesia—the collective body of believers who follow his lead and obey his commands. His desire is for us to grow together and love one another along the way. "By this all men will know that you are My disciples, if you have love for one another." We can only do this if we drop our competitive nature and embrace losing.

There is a significant difference in being an individual consumer of Christianity and a member of the body of Christ. Jesus prayed for all who would ever believe in him through his disciples' message, that we would all be one (John 17:20–21). The apostle Paul went to great lengths to explain this in several of his epistles by comparing being a part of Christ's body with being a human body part. He wrote, "The human body has many parts, but the many parts make up one whole body. So it is with the body of Christ" (1 Corinthians 12:12 NLT).

He continued:

> If the whole body were an eye, how would you hear? Or if your whole body were an ear, how would you smell anything? But our bodies have many parts, and God has put each part just where he wants it. How strange a body would be if it had only one part! Yes, there are many parts, but only one body. The eye can never say to the hand, "I don't need you." The head can't say to the feet, "I don't need you." This makes for harmony among the members, so that all the members care for each other. All of you together are Christ's body, and each of you is a part of it. (1 Corinthians 12:17–21, 25, 27 NLT)

Preston Sprinkle writes in his book *Go: Returning Discipleship to the Front Lines of Faith*, "To live out a Jesus-following faith—to be faithful disciples and be transformed into Christlikeness—we need other people. People to love, people to serve, people to relate to, argue with, forgive, enjoy, rebuke, and share our bread and wine with. *We can't do it by ourselves.*"

According to scripture, we cannot experience the fullness of God by ourselves. We need one another to love. We need authentic community and the collective gifts it possesses to grow. We must encourage each other to lose. Yes, we must become a collective bunch of losers!

Learning to lose is found in the pursuit of humility. When I began to truly pursue Christlikeness in my life, one area I greatly struggled with was pride. I wanted to win in everything. This characteristic was not easy to break. It was one thing to do this in my sports, but it carried over into all areas of my life.

Remember, I was so bad at this that some of my friends called me *Oge* (*ego* spelled backwards).

This nickname came several years into my pursuit of becoming more like Jesus, so clearly, I did not start taking on all of Jesus's characteristics in my life just because I desired to be more like him. Different areas of my life still needed repentance, but if we do not have a clear picture in mind of what we are becoming, there is no way we can become what we desire. This is where spending much time prayerfully reading my Bible and in fellowship with other believers became so critical. My friends sharpened me, and my time alone with God, reading his truths, began to transform me—because I wanted them to.

I wanted to be like Jesus, the manifestation of God in the flesh.

As I said earlier, humility was not natural for me, and my lack of it prevented me from embracing this central teaching of Jesus—to die to self. Therefore, I missed out on so much of what God wanted me to experience of him.

Several years ago, I decided to read the Bible all the way through, from start to finish. It seemed like a good idea until I got to Leviticus and Numbers. These books felt so dry and without meaningful application until I stumbled across a verse that forever changed my longing for humility. In Numbers 12, I discovered Aaron and Miriam (Moses's brother and sister) criticizing Moses. They said, "Has the Lord spoken only through Moses? Hasn't he spoken through us, too?" Then Numbers 12:3 says the most interesting thing in parentheses: "Now Moses was very humble—more humble than any other person on earth."

As I recalled, God did many amazing things through Moses, and I longed for God to use me in mighty ways as he did him. However, I realized when reading this passage that it was Moses's humility that gave him such clarity in following the Lord. I remember very clearly my aha moment: *God uses humble men.*

It was then that I began to pray for humility (I don't recommend this unless you are serious!), but God began to humble me, and humble me, and humble me—and he still is today. The result of being humbled was that God gave me eyes to see and ears to hear more of what he was up to around me. He showed me how to love others above myself and how he could work through me in that. It was from this mind-set that I could truly embrace the teachings of Jesus. I could finally embrace learning to lose!

"What you sow does not come to life unless it dies" (1 Corinthians 15:36). To live, we must die.

Galatians 2:20 says, "I have been crucified with Christ and I no longer live, but Christ lives in me. The life I now live in the body, I live by faith in the Son of God, who loved me and gave himself for me."

I think it's clear: To live as Christ, we must learn to die.

It took me years as a Christian to even begin to explore this foundational element of following Jesus in my own life because I wanted my plans *and* the glorious promises of Jesus. This dualism is the foundation of cultural Christianity but not Christ. Jesus was adamant that we could serve only one master.

DISCOVERING THE WORD

"Well, Josh, I guess every morning when I wake up, I just look forward to spending time with Jesus."

These were the words of my grandfather, Daddy Ray, in the last conversation I ever had with him from his hospice bed. It was his simple response, which I didn't fully understand at the time, to my question, "Daddy Ray, you've probably read everything in the Bible a dozen times. Why do you still read it every day?" As a twenty-six-year-old, I thought I knew most of what was in the Bible from my Christian education and from having grown up in church. I did not appreciate the beauty of his words until a few years later. Nonetheless, I will forever remember how this man of God helped me understand that we spend time with Jesus every time we open the scriptures.

Several years after receiving this indelible insight from my grandfather, I called a close friend of mine named Cole to get some career advice. I had been struggling for some time to raise enough financial support through my ministry to provide for my family, and I had recently started a side business where I was experiencing relational conflicts with my partners. I wanted wisdom from this successful real estate developer, of whom I thought highly, both professionally and personally. After laying out my situation to him, he said, "I don't know if I have any good career advice to offer you, but I do have one question: How much time are you spending reading your Bible and listening to God?"

I studied my Bible fairly often—after all, I was in ministry and taught Bible studies. For years, I used the Bible to inquire of God's perspective, gather information, affirm theology, explain Christian doctrine, teach, and share my knowledge with others, but there was something about his question that pierced my heart and reminded me of my Daddy Ray's words. I had never developed a long-term or consistent habit of spending time daily with Jesus, where my purpose was to listen to God and grow intimately with the person of Jesus through reading the words he gave us in scripture.

After a little more conversation with Cole, I agreed to make a commitment to spend an hour a day with God by listening to him as I read my Bible and prayed over its personal application to my life. Cole said he would call me the next week to see how I did.

Cole called on Friday and asked, "Did you get your time in?"

"I did," I replied.

"Tell me about it."

I had a lot to tell him. I was so excited, not just because I could brag about having spent more than six hours reading my Bible in a week but because I could share with him the things God had taught me. This process continued for a few weeks, and I truly fell in love with spending time with God while reading and taking notes on what God was saying to me personally through these ancient scriptures. Cole eventually recognized this time had become not only a habit but a craving for me, and he called me less often to check in. Now, several years later, I still check in with him from time to time for encouragement and a relational connection, but he never allows me to hang up without asking me if I am getting my time in each day. I cannot say that I don't miss a day here and there, but establishing the habit of spending time alone with the Lord in scripture has become my spiritual life source.

This is what my Daddy Ray was trying to tell me about his continued reading of scripture, even to his last day on earth. For many years, the Bible was an information source. Now when I open my Bible, I spend time connecting with Jesus through one of his greatest communication sources—scripture. I spend time with the one through whom all things were created and whose desire is to fill all things with himself.

Jesus is just as active now as he was two thousand years ago, when he physically walked on this earth. I have found that he actively moves when I read about that which he desires for me in his kingdom. He actively is engaged in my spirit, bringing about a healthy balance of encouragement and challenge. God uses the scriptures he preserved authentically, in combination with the Holy Spirit, to speak to my heart and mind.

All of scripture points toward our need for Jesus, and my eyes opened to things that I had never considered, even though I previously had read or studied most of what I was reading. The words had not changed, but my experience with them was significantly different. I could put heartfelt meaning and context to verses that I had memorized as a child. I found myself in the characters of the Old Testament stories, and when I read the Gospels, Acts of the Apostles, and the Epistles, I finally was discipled by Jesus. I fell in love with the person of Jesus, of whom I was gaining intimate knowledge and who Paul had explained so clearly. My Bible became my most prized possession.

When I was in high school, I memorized Romans 12:2 in Bible class. It says, "Do not conform to the pattern of this world, but be transformed by the renewing of your mind. Then, you will be able to test and approve what God's will is, his good, pleasing, and perfect will" (my memory version). For years I only understood the first part—not conforming to the ways of the world. I thought it meant that I must live the morality of a good Christian. It emboldened me to walk faithfully with God in certain areas of my life, but I never understood the "be transformed by the renewing of your mind" part, and I certainly did not always know God's will for me. Thankfully, I understand more of it now. It has become my life verse.

The Bible Is Not the Word

Discipleship of Jesus starts with our submission to his teachings and the writings of those who followed him. Many of us must first transform the way we think about the Bible itself before it can transform us. I always thought of the Bible as authoritative but not relational. If the Bible said it, I believed it, but it rarely moved me. It was like the US Constitution—timeless rules that never change that I must follow if I want to live in America, or in my case, be a good Christian. Now I see the scriptures in the Bible as a personal love letter from God to me.

All scripture points me toward the truth of who God is. I believe the Bible is the inspired witness to the true Word of God, Jesus Christ. I do not believe we should worship the Bible or put greater faith in the Bible than we do the living God. I have found, however, that the Bible not only validates everything Jesus stood for but is an incredible communication source from God so that we can live in an intimate and knowledgeable relationship with him.

I do not believe the Bible is necessary for us to have faith in Jesus and know the Lord, even though I love experiencing him through it. After all, the gospel spread from Jerusalem all around the Roman Empire, North Africa, and much of Asia for more than three hundred years, leading thousands to Jesus, before there was ever an officially canonized Bible. The Bible is not the foundation of our faith—Jesus is! The Bible validates our faith in Jesus and affirms what we claim about his life and teachings, just as my birth certificate, driver's license, and passport validate me. I do not exist because of them, but they give proof and verify facts about me.

We should look to scripture to understand and trust God's relentless pursuit of us, and we can experience God's communication with us as his dearly loved children. We should look to the scriptures to guide us in our walks with the Lord but not to be the source of our faith. The source is the living God, who exists with or without it. With that said, my Bible is my greatest treasure and source of wisdom, truth, and knowledge of the way to abundant life.

I do believe the Bible contains and preserves the words God spoke to man through the power of the Holy Spirit, but Jesus is the Word of God, and he is so much more than the words written about him on pages.

John began his Gospel with, "In the beginning was the Word, and the Word was with God, and the Word was God. He was with God in the beginning. Through him all things were made; without him nothing was made that has been made. In him was life, and that life was the light of all mankind. The Word became flesh and made his dwelling among us. We have seen his glory, the glory of the one and only Son, who came from the Father, full of grace and truth" (John 1:1–4, 14). He then concluded his Gospel with, "Jesus did many other things as well. If every one of them were written down, I suppose that even the whole world would not have room for the books that would be written" (John 21:25 NASB).

Just like I'm fine with you calling yourself a Christian, I'm fine if you want to keep calling the Bible the Word of God. His words are in there, but remember:

- The Word (*logos* in Greek) became flesh, not a book.
- Jesus is God. The Bible is not.
- The Bible did not create the heavens and earth; the Word did.
- We worship Jesus; we do not worship the Bible.
- The Bible does not have to exist or be inerrant for us to be saved, but Jesus had to.
- There is one mediator between God and man, and it's not the Bible—it's Jesus.

I emphasize this because many Christians practice biblicism today. The Bible is the foundation to their faith. Biblicists often put the Bible as more foundational than the relational God who inspired the men who wrote it. They often place these men, who, like us, were in a continual growth process in their knowledge of God, as more esteemed than the power of the Holy Spirit given to each of us. I believe every book of the Bible to be canon (pass the test) and authorized by God, to be kept, preserved, and cherished for all generations. The Bible, however, is not the foundation of my faith; Jesus is.

God interacted and spoke with men like Adam, Noah, Abraham, Isaac, Jacob, and Moses before a single piece of scripture was ever written. The book of Hebrews says that Abraham was made righteous in God's sight because of his faith. Among many other faithful men, God continued to reveal himself progressively to the likes of Job, David, and Hezekiah, but these men had no assurance that upon their death they would continue in the presence of God. They were disheartened by the thought of going to the grave (*sheol* in Hebrew and *Hades* in Greek, also translated as the realm or place of the dead).

> Who rejoice greatly, and exult when they find the grave? (Job 3:22 NASB)

> Turn, Lord, and deliver me; save me because of your unfailing love. Among the dead no one proclaims your name. Who praises you from the grave? (Psalm 6:4–5 NIV)

> What will you gain if I die, if I sink into the grave? Can my dust praise you? Can it tell of your faithfulness? (Psalm 30:9 NLT)

> The heavens belong to the LORD, but he has given the earth to all humanity. The dead cannot sing praises to the LORD, for they have gone into silence of the grave. (Psalm 115:16–17 NLT)

For the dead cannot praise you; they cannot raise their voices in praise. Those who go down to the grave can no longer hope in your faithfulness. Only the living can praise you as I do today. Each generation tells of your faithfulness to the next. (Isaiah 38:17-18 NLT)

These men may have hoped for a future resurrection and restoration of their souls, but they had no assurance of being in the relational presence of God when they died. This concept was radically introduced by Jesus.

The Bible reveals that God eternally interacts with his most prized creation in a way that far surpasses our ability to derive our entire theology from the words of his inspired scriptures alone.

Our faith should never conflict with scripture, when understood in its proper context. We must engage God individually and corporately and expect scripture to clarify and direct us to what we are to believe. The scriptures of the Bible are amazing! We should praise God for them and delight in them. They validate and correct everything we know of God's character and his relational interaction with us. Human words, however, cannot fully encompass the Alpha and Omega. God is greater than the texts that tell us about him. Intimate knowledge of Jesus and his love, grace, and mercy far surpasses deep intellectual knowledge of scripture.

Jesus is the Word, and he "is living and active and sharper than any two-edged sword" (Hebrews 4:12 NASB). God pursues each one of us in a personal and collective way. He uses scripture as a powerful means to do so, but he is not limited to scripture alone.

He did not use scripture to convert Saul of Tarsus. He met him personally on the road to Damascus.

God is relational, and he reveals himself to us in many ways. He is constantly at work in each of us, drawing us into a closer relationship with him and each other. The Word of God comes in many forms, yet it's always consistent.

If anything I've written in this chapter about the Word of God or the Bible challenges your Christian doctrine, I ask that you prayerfully bring God into it. My only agenda is to glorify God. Only through reading my Bible and my devotion to spending time with Jesus to know him fully did the words of scripture and the Holy Spirit's interaction with me challenge my own previously existing claims. You may not agree with my assertions, but use the scriptures, in context, as your defense. The Bible uses the phrase *the Word of God* often. I have never found that it makes the claims about itself that Christians do.

Let me be clear: I am not making any claims against the inspiration, canonization, or infallibility of the Bible. I believe every author wrote as he was inspired to do by the Holy Spirit.

Logically, I could even argue that if one perceives areas of inconsistencies—especially in minute details or in perfect accuracy of order, times of the day, dates, numbers, and which people were present at some events—this should strengthen, not weaken, one's faith. This would be especially true for the Gospels, as they pertain to eyewitness accounts. Often a jury in a trial is instructed that if they recognize subtle differences in witness testimonies, that it is a good thing because it proves there is no conspiracy or collusion taking place.

God wants us to know him, and if there happens to be slight errors in recorded details or in translation, the Bible we have today completely passes the test of jurisprudence and can be fully trusted to assist us in knowing the Word of God.

Again, I don't make these points to frustrate you but to suggest that we should not fill in the gaps or add to scripture to satisfy our doctrinal claims. God does not need us to defend him. In many ways, our doing so minimizes his sovereignty and our dependence on the one thing we know to be perfect—the living, active, relational, and eternal God.

The authors of the Bible refer to Jesus as the Word. It is written in scripture that he existed long before the scriptures were ever written.

So instead of saying the Bible is the Word of God, we should make the same claim that John did in the opening chapter of his Gospel: "In the beginning was the Word, and the Word was with God, and the Word was God. He was in the beginning with God. All things came into being through Him, and apart from Him nothing came into being that has come into being. In Him was life, and the life was the Light of men. The Light shines in the darkness, and the darkness did not comprehend it" (John 1:1–5 NASB).

So, then, what is the Word of God? It is the communication of God. The Word existed from the beginning, and it continues as the communication link between God and individuals today. Scripture is an important part of what God uses to communicate with us, but so is Jesus, the holy one who manifested God to man. God has used—and still uses—many methods to speak. He continues to use the Holy Spirit, prophecy, and other ways to communicate his plans for us in his kingdom, just as he did when the original scriptures were first recorded.

Broccoli in My Teeth

Most Christians have heard the verse, "Do not point out the splinter [sawdust] in your neighbor's eye when there is a plank [log] in your own eye." Christians accept this as good correction for being judgmental. Rarely do we take the next step of looking in the mirror to examine what is interfering with our own vision. We may try not to judge, but I think Jesus wants us to deal with the splinter that is blinding us.

People usually think their own worldview is normal, but many of us don't want to address our natural tendencies that are contrary to the way of Jesus. Yes, we all have personality styles—some of us are more direct and challenging, and some of us are naturally more supportive and agreeable. According to the Myers-Briggs Type Indicator, we are introverts or extroverts, sensors or intuitives, feelers or thinkers, and judgers or perceivers. Personality and type assessments can be very helpful in understanding our natural tendencies in how we deal with people relationally, process information, make decisions, and operate in work environments or social settings. Some types are more inclined to tradition and others to innovation. Some take what they're taught at face value, some challenge, and some want to dig deeper. We have varied tendencies when dealing with and responding to God as well.

Jesus was part of the creation process, so he knows how we operate. He gets us, and he leads us—regardless of our tendencies or personality type—into his likeness. We all must spend time looking in the mirror, examining ourselves, so we know that the sawdust in our eyes is keeping us from seeing how to live and love in his kingdom.

I like to call this the broccoli in our teeth. It's like when you've been at a party for a couple of hours and only realize when you go to the restroom that an ugly green thing has been hanging from your teeth every time you smile (I can't help but think of Jim Carrey in *Ace Ventura*, hanging the asparagus from his teeth), but nobody was bold enough to tell you. Fortunately for us, the Holy Spirit is never afraid to let us know about the broccoli in our teeth that Jesus came to address—the problem is, we often don't listen to his still, quiet voice. We are too busy, distracted, and consumed with the things of this world. Moreover, many of us are not engaged in true, authentic community that's committed to sharpen us through love and grace and is balanced in support and challenge.

Jesus wasn't afraid to point out the broccoli in the Pharisees' teeth either, but they too didn't want to listen. I have a feeling that many of the onlookers were elbowing their neighbors and giving fist bumps every time Jesus called out the religious leaders for their hypocrisy, pride, and arrogance, but the leaders were too pious to accept his admonition. Today, cultural Christians have done the same thing.

Most of us have become good actors in our religious and spiritual circles, but rarely do we look intently in the mirror and invite Jesus into the areas of our lives that he still wants to address. And if we get enough false endorsement from those around us, eventually our hearts become callous, and we stop trying to grow spiritually. We move all our spiritual work into our heads and actions but rarely into our hearts.

We may become more knowledgeable of the Bible to develop sound doctrine, but we focus it outwardly. We tell the homosexual community they are an abomination to God; we take a firm stance against abortion; and we take other positions of moral authority, which are not necessarily bad positions in and of themselves, but we don't address our own inward sins before we judge the rest of the world.

This was the situation in which Jesus found himself when the religious leaders brought a woman caught in adultery before him; they were ready to stone her. The Pharisees wanted to test Jesus to see if they had grounds for accusing him of not following God's law (John 8). Jesus had no broccoli in his teeth, but he had many students and onlookers who did, so, in his wisdom and love, he responded beautifully. Jesus stooped down and began to write on the ground. We don't know what he was writing, but some ascertain that he might have been writing the different sins of his accusers. (I think he was playing tic-tac-toe with Bartholomew.) Regardless of what he wrote, we can all learn from his verbal response: "He who is without sin among you, let him be the first to throw a stone at her" (John 8:7 NASB). Jesus could have judged the world, but he did not come to do that; rather, he came to save it. One by one, the religious leaders walked away.

Jesus then confronted the woman, as no one had condemned her. "I do not condemn you, either. Go. From now on sin no more" (John 8:11 NASB). Jesus never condones any sin, but he understands that we are all works in progress. Pastor or congregation member, believer or nonbeliever, Catholic or Protestant—we all need to examine ourselves first before accusing others. (Although being an Auburn fan, I think I am permitted to pass judgment on an Alabama fan.)

Jesus came to empower life change, and he did that with the adulterous woman. He did not let her off the hook, but she needed to know the Savior of the world was 100 percent for her. He supported her when no one else did, and then he challenged her to leave behind her sinful ways.

This is an example for all of us. This is how the body of Christ should conduct themselves. Because we believe something is wrong doesn't give us the right to be the judge; we are all works in the progress. The adulterous woman appears to have accepted this. It was the prideful religious men who did not.

It is not the healthy who need a doctor, but the sick.
(Luke 5:31 NIV)

This is a lesson for Christians today: We must examine our own hearts before we attack the rest of the world. The longer I look in the mirror, the more I realize how much Jesus is at work in me. I find comfort that the apostle Paul, well into his ministry, felt the same way I do. Not only did Paul recognize that in his past he was "the foremost of all [sinners]" (1 Timothy), but in his letter to the Romans, he referred to himself as being a "wretched man."

Paul was striving for Christlikeness; he refused to settle for anything less. Even though he claimed that he was worthy of being imitated because he was imitating the Lord, he never stopped pursuing the completion Christ had set out before him as his ultimate destiny. He refused to wait for death to be freed of his strongholds. He wanted to experience all of God in this life.

The tendency in Christianity is to evaluate ourselves based on moral relativism and not on Jesus's teaching. For example, in many conservative churches, any form of alcohol consumption is wrong and judged, but overeating and obesity is acceptable. Potentially, people who consume wine or beer just as responsibly as (we can assume) Jesus did are judged by their church, but the pastor and elders can neglect their bodies in many other ways and still be considered model Christians. We have made things sinful that even Jesus did, but we have minimized things that matter to God.

Cultural Christianity says our families should be our top priority, and it greatly praises worldly accomplishments and financial success, but Jesus said, "If anyone comes to Me, and does not hate [by comparison of his love for Me] his own father and mother and wife and children and brothers and sisters, yes, and even his own life, he cannot be My disciple. So then, none of you can be My disciple who does not give up all his own possessions" (Luke 14:26, 33 NASB).

I do not believe this means that we must be poor and homeless and abandon families and responsibilities to follow Jesus. I do believe, though, that we must learn to prize the kingdom of God above the things of this world.

Since the kingdom of God is centered around our relationship with God and our relationships with others, we should value our relationships with our spouses and families above what we can do for them by obtaining financial security or making priceless memories together.

We think creating avenues for success and enjoyment is love, but true love requires fighting for the best possible outcome in the life of another. We must fight for an eternal perspective for them. If we are more focused on providing the "blessings" of this world, it is quite possible that we are creating obstacles for them to advance in the kingdom of God.

Jesus taught that "it is harder for a rich man to enter the Kingdom of God than for a camel to go through the eye of a needle." Thankfully, he did say next that "nothing is impossible for God." It is imperative to understand that the kingdom of God requires dependence on him, not self. Self-reliance is our greatest hindrance to living as Christ.

"Blessed are the poor in spirit, for theirs is the Kingdom of Heaven"—Matthew quotes Jesus's opening line in the Sermon on the Mount. Poor in spirit is the opposite of self-reliance. Christians often have the tendency, just as the Pharisees did, of directing self-reliance and performance-based work as the means of executing their beliefs.

Jesus modeled dependency on the Holy Spirit to do what the Father willed, and so too should we. "I am the vine, you are the branches; he who abides in Me and I in him, he bears much fruit, for apart from Me you can do nothing" (John 15:5).

On our own, we cannot get the broccoli out of our teeth and begin producing spiritual fruit.

The wonderful things of this world can easily replace God's will as our priorities. The kingdom of this world gets in the way of our walking together deeper in Christ and leading each other further into the kingdom of God. The central purpose of Jesus's ministry was to make his kingdom available and lead his followers into it. He greatly emphasized that we cannot love this world *and* him. The things of this world can distract us from our greater purpose and from that which lasts for eternity. By pursuing him and his kingdom, we then become better lovers of each other. We must be careful of thinking that when we better our family's circumstances that we are loving them best. That goes for loving ourselves as well.

One of the areas I had to address in my own heart was my love for the things of this world. I did not pursue success eternally, but it was for selfish ambition and vain conceit. I viewed financial giving as a spiritual accomplishment, as if I could impress God with how much money I gave to charitable organizations. I wanted to further his kingdom, but I did not understand how it operated. I saw it through a worldly lens, just as I viewed myself and my shortcomings. Discovering the broccoli in our teeth requires a kingdom-of-God lens. Without gaining *eyes to see*, as Jesus has and desires to give us, we usually only look in the mirror at our actions and not at our character. Changing behavior is easy; gaining the character of God is a much longer and harder process.

My concern is for how Christians address cultural issues and make stances against things in society. We see this prominently in the way Christians address sexual sin. Many churches would not welcome a homosexual couple to attend their church services, but they would allow a heterosexual couple who is living together out of wedlock. (We would even rush them down the aisle to marry them, as if that would remove their sin.) Jesus addressed all sins, and he can remove all sin from our lives with our submission. All sexual sins are outside God's design. They are harmful and not meant for the body of Christ, but we must be careful that we do not address them differently based on cultural acceptance.

I do not bring up any of these moral issues to take a social stance on obesity, alcohol consumption, or human sexuality (that is for another time and place, when I know my audience is submitted to

Christ); rather, I want to point out that we have become selective in our pursuit of God's plan for us, based on Christian culture's emphasis. Jesus took great exception with the Pharisees on this.

For instance, the Pharisees made the tradition of ceremonially washing their hands before they ate a spiritual matter, and they criticized Jesus's disciples for not obeying their cultural traditions. The Pharisees didn't know the difference between what had become a cultural tradition and a pursuit of spiritual righteousness. They had replaced that which was easy to do with that which was not. Washing their hands before they ate was much easier than cleansing their hearts of pride, lust, greed, anger, and jealousy. Humility no longer was a virtue, and pride was perfectly acceptable.

We live in a society today where Christian culture praises wealth and financial success. In fact, we usually make the wealthiest and most successful men in our church the elders. We label individuals who support our ministries and write large checks to our capital campaigns as generous, without knowing the percentage of their incomes that they gave, but we overlook the dedication of the lower-middle-class family that tithes, serves, and prays faithfully for their local congregation. My point is that we must not allow cultural Christianity to determine the benchmark Jesus set.

As mentioned repeatedly, I, on my own power and will, satisfied all the Christian standards of an adolescent and young man, yet I grew less and less sensitive to Christ's agenda for me and the people God had placed in my life. I had many splinters in my eyes and much broccoli in my teeth. I was completely unaware because I was not being discipled in the way of Jesus. I was simply conforming to the patterns of Christian culture. In many parts of America, particularly the Bible Belt, we can "conform to the patterns of this world" and be praised as a good Christian. We must be brave enough to look below the surface, deeper into the mirror, and into our hearts to examine if we are growing in the way of culture or the way of Jesus.

You may find, as I did, that the Christian culture into which you are assimilating is not a Christlike culture at all; it only bears his name.

GOD'S BELOVED

"You like me. You really like me!" is the oft misquoted line from Sally Field's acceptance speech for Best Actress at the 1985 Academy Awards. What she really said was, "I can't deny the fact that you like me; right now, you like me!" Regardless of the accuracy of how it is remembered, this is the kind of acceptance that God wants all his children to know from him. Our ability to love God and others is directly proportionate to our ability to receive and accept God's love for us.

The problem for me, for most of my life, was that I did not feel liked by God. I knew God loved me because scripture says he does. I figured that he was obligated to love me, but I never felt that God was very fond of me. I always felt like I disappointed him. I didn't measure up to his expectations, so that was why most of my prayers went unanswered.

I understood God forgave me of my sins, once and for all, because of my belief in his Son, but when I read my Bible or heard scripture quoted, I only saw what I was supposed to do to be a better Christian. I tried so hard to do those things, but I did not feel that I ever earned God's favor. I found life getting harder and more painful, rather than easier and more joyful. I did not know the freedom that is supposed to be found in Christ. I felt enslaved by the religion of Christianity, and I was worn out from trying to be a "human doing," rather than resting in him as his beloved human being.

I had fallen into a pit of despair. Pulling out the splinters from my eye was painful. I wanted desperately to address the sin in my life. I was disgusted by my pride and desire to always come out on top. I so badly wanted to become the man God wanted me to be—a true follower of Christ. I had become so hyper-focused on my shortcomings that I could not embrace God's love. I addressed the sin in my life the same way I built up these areas of ugliness—on my own. I did not invite Jesus into the healing; instead, I tried to perform miracles on myself. I began to struggle greatly with depression. I wanted so much to do the will of God but felt nothing but hopelessness and despair. I struggled to fund my ministry and to financially provide for my family. I tried desperately to do the work of God, but I felt like a complete failure. The more I thought I was growing, the harder life became.

At just the right time, a mentor came into my life named Jim Hiskey. Jim was focused on raising up and multiplying disciples of Jesus, just as I thought I was, but he had forty-three more years of experience than I had at making mistakes. Over recent years, Jim had developed some foundational questions for discipleship, with scripted answers from the Bible. One of these particularly was key to my ability to move forward.

"Josh, what is the *work* of the Lord?"

Well, Jim, if I knew that, I probably wouldn't be struggling to fund my ministry and see lots of fruitful success! I thought.

I was instructed to open my Bible and read John 6:28–29. I read aloud: "Therefore, they said to Him, 'What shall we do, so that we may work the works of God?' Jesus answered and said to them, 'This is the work of God, that you believe in Him whom He has sent.'"

As we began to talk deeply about this passage, I realized that the foundation of all my growth in Jesus and all the good things that I wanted to do in his name had been dependent on my efforts. Yet I knew that everything good must be performed by him.

Our job is to cooperate with what he is doing. I can do nothing to bear fruit in the kingdom of God without his authorization and outpouring of grace. Jesus claimed that "he did nothing on his own will, but he only did the will of his Heavenly Father," and that came from the Son of God, and "all things were created through him."

As mentioned in the previous chapter, Jesus modeled to us how to depend on God for everything. Therefore, if Jesus depended on heaven as he performed his ministry, how much more dependent did I need to be on him to accomplish anything good?

Again, the Sermon on the Mount begins, "Blessed are the poor in spirit, for they will inherit the Kingdom of Heaven." For years I thought Jesus was trying to make the downtrodden feel better, but when I equated *poor in spirit* with dependency on God, my perspective began to change.

This alone was not life-changing, but it led to a series of eye-opening realizations that I like to refer to as *lens changes*. A lens change is the process of seeing things more clearly, as heaven already knows it to be. It is gradual and progressive. We never have a final, fully mature lens change in this life, even though that is the course we are traveling. *Following Jesus is a journey of growth; the Christianity I had been taught was a place of arrival.* My Pharisee mentality was incapable of receiving lens changes because the performance–focus mind-set sees a scorecard. Remember, I was a "good Christian" in my youth, but I did not pursue spiritual growth. Instead, I chased accomplishments and recognition to satisfy my ego, but God had something better in mind—humility.

Jesus often called the Pharisees and other teachers of the Law *blind*; he told them that they could not see the kingdom of God. Learning to live in God's kingdom is a process of mind transformation. God desires to give us new sets of kingdom lenses as he continues to renew our minds through the process of discipleship of Jesus.

Jesus said, "Can the blind lead the blind? Will they not both fall into a pit? The student is not above the teacher, but everyone who is fully trained will be like their teacher."

The blindness and Phariseeism that I had developed was

theologically sound Christianity, but I did not know the joy and intimacy of God. My Christian environments were good, and I tried to be the best I could be in them. Well into my journey of what I thought was true Christianity, I fell into a pit too deep for me to climb out on my own. Shedding my performance mind-set was necessary but not easy because I never truly believed God was proud of me. I saw growth in Christlike areas and learned to love others better as I crucified parts of my old self, but I also lost self-esteem and identity. I still did not like the man in the mirror, and I needed to hear from God that he did. I asked my heavenly Father to tell me what he really thought of me, and this led to one of the most important breakthroughs of my life.

My friend Cole recommended a spiritual healing retreat in Missouri that he and his wife had attended. He did not tell me much about what to expect on the retreat, except that he was confident that God would show up right where I needed him. Without hesitation and mostly out of despair, I signed up and went on their next retreat.

We all have wounds that we carry from our past that our spiritual enemy uses to attack us. I'm sure I have more than I realize, but the one that I recognize most comes from my belief that if I do not achieve in a noteworthy manner or at an exceptional level, then I am of no value. My natural personality would lend itself to this line of thinking, but then if you consider that my father is a World Golf Hall of Fame member who has been a recognizable name on the PGA Tour and PGA Tour Champions throughout my entire life, you can see how Satan could work to deceive me about my identity in Christ. By the time my father was my age, he had already won three of professional golf's major championships; I was struggling just to provide for my family and be happy with my life.

To my dad's credit, he never said anything that I can recall that reinforced this wound. Rather, the enemy used the systems of this world and the people of it to shoot my heart with his arrows. As a senior in high school, I was trying to decide between two large Southeastern Conference universities to attend when the one I was leaning against sent me a very nice academic scholarship offer. That did not help my decision-making process, so the next day I spoke with my high school guidance counselor to get her thoughts. I asked her why she thought that school had given me the scholarship, and she so thoughtfully replied, "They probably just found out who your dad is."

I did not realize at the time that her words were an arrow into my heart, and so I carried them with me for years. I never invited God to heal the wound. Instead of letting him pull out the arrow and pour truth into the wound, I held on to it.

I once played in a big national junior golf tournament, and did not play very well the first round. After spending some time practicing after the round, I went over to check the leader board to see where I stood, as compared to the rest of the field. It just so happened I was standing next to a father and son who didn't know me but knew of me. I overheard the father say to his son, "Josh Nelson. That's Larry Nelson's son. You'd think he'd be better than that!"

These were not isolated incidents. My whole life, even in adulthood, I have received comments, probably never intended to hurt me, that have reinforced my belief that I was of no value if I did not accomplish extraordinary things. To this day, instead of being introduced to people for who I am, I am very often introduced by acquaintances in the following manner: "[So-and-so], meet Josh Nelson. You probably know who his dad is ..."

For years these comments were arrows the enemy was using to damage my heart. Do you know the ways the enemy has targeted your heart?

Are the arrows still in there?

Have you ever let Jesus heal the wound?

Praise the Lord, after much wrestling with God and my emotions on the retreat, God encountered me through his messenger, the Holy Spirit, several days into it. In one of the teaching sessions, we were presented a piece of scripture in a beautiful way; I had known the scripture my entire life, but I'd never seen myself in it. It's the story of the disciple Peter's three denials of Jesus during his trial. We don't know if Jesus audibly heard any of the denials, but he certainly knew, as he had already predicted it over dinner. The story does not end as I remembered it, with Peter breaking down and weeping, having to forever live with the shame of being the disciple who denied following Jesus. That is not his legacy.

In Mark's Gospel, he shines a little light on Jesus's desire to heal our emotional and spiritual wounds. After the resurrection, Mark wrote something odd—unless you consider his close friendship with Peter and hear the story through his lens. When the women discovered the empty tomb of Jesus early on Easter morning, they were met by an angel, who said to them, "He is risen from the dead! Look, this is where they laid his body. Now go and tell his disciples, including Peter, that Jesus is going ahead of you to Galilee. You will see him there, just as he told you before he died" (Mark 16:6–7 NLT).

Including Peter! You mean the one who denied three times that he even knew Jesus just days before?

The messenger of the Lord mentioned Peter with intentionality, as if he wanted to make sure Peter knew that he was not removed from God's good graces because of his cowardly denial of his Son and lack of belief in all that he'd gone through over the last three years. We then find an amazing interaction with Jesus and Peter at Galilee in the Gospel of John that completes the story of Jesus's nursing Peter's wound. The disciples had been out fishing in a boat all night but had caught nothing. At dawn, a man standing on the beach called out to them, "Have you caught any fish?" (John 21:5 NLT).

They replied no, so he instructed them to throw their net out on the other side of their boat and told them they would get some fish. It says they caught so many fish that they couldn't haul in the net. This is when they realized it was the Lord, and immediately

Peter jumped off the boat and raced to shore. When he got to shore, breakfast was waiting for all of them.

> So when they had finished breakfast, Jesus said to Simon Peter, "Simon, son of John, do you love Me more than these?" He said to Him, "Yes, Lord; You know that I love You." He said to him, "Tend My lambs." He said to him again a second time, "Simon, son of John, do you love Me?" He said to Him, "Yes, Lord; You know that I love You." He said to him, "Shepherd My sheep." He said to him the third time, "Simon, son of John, do you love Me?" Peter was grieved because He said to him the third time, "Do you love Me?" And he said to Him, "Lord, You know all things; You know that I love You." Jesus said to him, "Tend My sheep." (John 21:15–17 NASB)

Jesus used this redemptive conversation to restore Peter's heart and to empower him to lead the body of Christ in Jerusalem and eventually have an amazing ministry around the Roman Empire. Jesus knew exactly what Peter's heart needed to be healed and made even stronger than before. It was the personal experience of the resurrected Jesus that empowered and emboldened Peter into having an amazing, world-changing ministry for the next thirty-plus years. He also used this story to speak into and heal my heart. *I was finally convinced that I was worth pursuing!*

At any point in my life, Jesus would have done for me what he did for Peter, if I'd been ready to receive it,. He actively went to the same lengths to redeem my heart.

God answered my greatest desire of him; he told me what he thought of me. I was not a disappointment or a failure, overlooked and forgotten by God, as I had come to falsely believe. Rather, I was his beloved child. I was Joshua, purposefully given the same name as his son, Yeshua. Joshua and Jesus are both from the Hebrew name Yeshua or Yahshua, which means "Yahweh [God] is savior." From conception, giving me the name of his Son, God always desired for me to know that I have always been cherished and pursued by him. My performance does not affect his fondness of me. He intends for me to know and receive all of him, holding nothing of heaven back, so I can give him away to others.

My doubts and false beliefs from my own experiences and wounds were not true. What was true about me was not the truth about me! It is true that I have past failures, just like Peter, but the truth is that "there is now no condemnation for those in Christ Jesus," and he has given me all that I need to live victoriously in his kingdom and tend to his sheep.

Understanding the Gospel

> If you believe what you like in the gospels, and reject what you don't like, it is not the gospel you believe, but yourself.
>
> —Saint Francis

As mentioned frequently in this book, Christianity today is a far migration from what Jesus taught his disciples to do once they received the power of the Holy Spirit. Dick Halverson, longtime chaplain of the United States Senate, put it this way: "In the beginning the church was a fellowship of men and women centering on the living Christ. Then the church moved to Greece where it became a philosophy. Then it moved to Rome where it became an institution. Next, it moved to Europe, where it became a culture. And, finally, it moved to America where it became an enterprise."

Christianity evolved into a religion over several centuries, eventually becoming a conglomerate of many denominations, doctrines, and practices that has adherents who know very little of the teachings of the so-called founder of it. Most Christians believe in Jesus's death and resurrection as their source of salvation, but they commonly pick and choose what they like from the things Jesus taught and commanded.

That was my approach for many years as well.

When I became serious about reading the Bible on a dedicated and consistent basis, I spent a lot of time immersed in the four

Gospels. I wanted to know the person of Jesus so that I could reflect his character and follow him completely. It did not take me long to realize that what I had prioritized and known, even though sound in most Christian circles, was challenged by what I read in scripture.

First, I did not really know the teachings of Jesus. I had never seen myself as one of his disciples. Disciples were the men who were willing to give up everything to blindly follow Jesus and later learn why. I already knew what Jesus had done for me, and I accepted it; therefore, I did not see their apprenticeship as something to be replicated for spiritual growth. Second, I had never known there was an underlying theme to everything Jesus taught—the kingdom of God I knew nothing about. I knew the stories of Jesus and his disciples, but I did not get the purpose of their learning process.

Jesus was teaching them a process they should replicate, as he eventually commissioned them to make disciples of all nations and to teach them everything he had taught them. This was to continue until he returns.

I knew the stories; I had what I thought was sound doctrine, and I could quote many verses from scripture. I knew of John the Baptist, Jesus's cousin, who was the one who announced the arrival of the promised Messiah and was baptizing people to "Make ready the way of the Lord" (Matthew 3:2 NASB), but I never really thought much about what he was saying—"Repent, for the kingdom of heaven is at hand" (Matthew 3:3 NASB). After John introduced and baptized Jesus, Jesus began his ministry with the same message. From that time, Jesus began to preach and say, "Repent, for the kingdom of heaven is at hand" (Matthew 4:17 NASB).

Luke writes that as Jesus began teaching, healing the sick, and casting out demons in his hometown of Nazareth of Galilee, the people did not want him to leave, "but he said to them, 'I must preach the kingdom of God to the other cities also, for I was sent for this purpose'" (Luke 4:43 NASB).

Mark makes it even clearer in his Gospel, as he opens his account of Jesus ministry with, "Now after John had been taken into custody,

Jesus came into Galilee, preaching the gospel of God, and saying, 'The time is fulfilled, and the kingdom of God is at hand; repent and believe in the gospel'" (Mark 1:14–15 NASB).

I started to notice a trend—the gospel of Jesus was preached, and it had nothing to do with the resurrection yet. Not only that, but he was turning people away from religion and was replacing a human-derived methodology with something new and different. He was not teaching Religion 2.0: The Love and Grace Version.

The gospel was and still is a person—Jesus. His purpose was to usher in the kingdom of God. The kingdom of God remains the topic of discussion and focus for the remainder of the Gospels and is the theme of the apostles' teaching throughout Acts and in the Epistles. Jesus continued to proclaim and preach the kingdom of God with his disciples and to all the towns he visited.

As the crowds grew with both skeptics and believers, Jesus began teaching in parables, and nearly every one of them starts with, "The kingdom of heaven is like …" or "The kingdom of God is like …"

He frequently said, "He who has ears to hear, let him hear," suggesting that they did not accurately understand what he was talking about.

The process of discipleship is to bring us into maturity, where we gain full understanding of the kingdom of God. Jesus said, "Everyone, after he has been fully trained, will be like his teacher" (Luke 6:40 NASB). If I was on a journey to be transformed into the likeness of Christ, then I would have to become a student of his.

When Jesus's disciples questioned him about the meaning of a parable, he said, "To you it has been granted to know the mysteries of the kingdom of God, but to the rest it is in parables, so that seeing they may not see, and hearing they may not hear" (Luke 8:9–10 NASB). Then, he explained the meaning to them. Even though they did not yet fully understand the meaning of it, Jesus sent them out to proclaim the kingdom of God and perform healing. Not too long afterward, he said something that really got my attention: "But I say to you truthfully, there are some of those standing here who will not taste death until they see the kingdom of God" (Luke 9:27 NASB).

Jesus was saying that the kingdom of God would come in the lifetime of these disciples, which means the kingdom of God is already here. Granted, there are some things that are yet to come, but as Jesus said when he began his ministry, it was his purpose. He would eventually go to the cross to make this purpose a reality, but he had much to say about it before his death. After his resurrection, he appeared to them "over a period of forty days and speaking of the things concerning the kingdom of God" (Acts 1:3 NASB).

The kingdom of God was unknown and a mystery to those listening, but as Jesus said,

> The Law and the Prophets were proclaimed until John [the Baptist]; since that time the gospel of the kingdom of God has been preached, and everyone is forcing his way into it. (Luke 16:16)

> Enter through the narrow gate; for the gate is wide and the way is broad that leads to destruction, and there are many [so-called Christian] who enter through it. For the gate is small and the way is narrow that leads to life, and there are few who find it … Unless one is born again he cannot see the kingdom of God. (Matthew 7:13–14; John 3:3 NASB)

I had claimed to be a born-again Christian since I was six years old, but I still could not see the kingdom of God. As it turns out, I was an infant in the kingdom into which I was born. I had not been led into healthy growth in the kingdom that God intended to give me when I accepted him into my heart at a young age. Cultural Christianity had not led me into God's kingdom; it had led me into a self-reliant, theologically sound, sin-managed Christian lifestyle that produced very little fruit.

I wanted to be a hundredfold producer in the kingdom of God, but I did not know what it looked like. I desired to do the work of the Lord, but I did not understand that it required dependence on him to do so. Jesus modeled this to the disciples, but nobody had ever modeled it to me. I had only been taught what it looked like to be a good Christian. I had received the Christian gospel, but I desired to be a disciple of Jesus so that I could know the full gospel of God.

Once again, I return to Jesus's explanation of the kingdom of God to his disciples through the Parable of the Sower:

> Now the parable is this: the seed is the word of God. Those beside the road are those who have heard; then the devil comes and takes away the word from their heart, so that they will not believe and be saved. Those on the rocky soil are those who, when they hear, receive the word with joy; and these have no firm root; they believe for a while, and in time of temptation fall away. The seed which fell among the thorns, these are the ones who have heard, and as they go on their way they are choked with worries and riches and pleasures of this life, and bring no fruit to maturity. But the seed in the good soil, these are the ones who have heard the word in an honest and good heart, and hold it fast, and bear fruit with perseverance. (Luke 8:11–15 NASB)

Where do you find yourself in this parable?

My concern with Christianity, as it is taught and lived out in our culture, is the way we address the soils. The first soil is often evangelized, but because we lack the discipleship culture that Jesus commanded, many are never led into a believing walk with the Lord, and so they fall away. As for the rocky-soil individuals, many

Christians are offered a gospel of salvation but are not presented with a foundation of the true gospel of Jesus's lordship over their lives. Therefore, when they face trials and temptations, they either turn to self-reliance or give in and place their eternal hope on the safety net of the partial gospel they knew.

Most frequently, we settle for the third soil because very few of us have been immersed in the kingdom of God in our Christian environments. Christianity, as it has become, allows for the serving of two masters, and it does not lead us into the fullness of the kingdom of God. It compromises Jesus's teachings and fails to teach against the love of this world. The weeds and thorns of this world grow alongside the good plant and choke out what was meant for maturity and completion. We often hear sermons and read books on how to be better at living the Christian life, not realizing we are promoting how to further ourselves in the kingdom of the world in a Christian way.

Jesus warned us of this in many ways. He said, "For whoever wishes to save his life will lose it, but whoever loses his life for My sake, he is the one who will save it. For what is a man profited if he gains the whole world, and loses or forfeits himself?" (Luke 9:24–25 NASB).

He said in the Sermon on the Mount,

> "Every tree that does not bear good fruit is cut down and thrown into the fire. So then, you will know them by their fruits. Not everyone who says to me Lord, Lord,' will enter the kingdom of heaven, but he who does the will of My Father who is in heaven will enter. Many will say to Me on that day, 'Lord, Lord, did we not prophesy in Your name, and in Your name cast out demons, and in Your name perform many miracles?' And then I will declare to them, 'I never knew you; depart from Me, you who practice lawlessness.'" (Matthew 7:18–23 NASB)

If we are focused more on finding success, happiness, and living good and comfortable lives than on how God may produce eternal fruit through us, then we should be concerned.

Success in this world is not an indication of eternal fruit being produced. Instead, Jesus taught that it most often is an obstacle to it. Not only are power, wealth, and influence roadblocks to the Way, but so is getting our priorities out of whack.

We must be careful of worshiping anything above God, including our families. "He who loves father or mother more than Me is not worthy of Me; and he who loves son or daughter more than Me is not worthy of Me. He who has found his life will lose it, and he who has lost his life for My sake will find it" (Matthew 10:37–39). We find very little on parenting and marriage in the Bible and much on being disciples of Jesus. Christian bookstores, however, are full of the former and greatly lacking in material on authentic Christlike discipleship.

One of the greatest books I have ever read is Dallas Willard's *The Great Omission: Reclaiming Jesus's Essential Teachings on Discipleship.* He points out how the very thing Jesus trained and sent his disciples out to do is missing from modern-day Christianity. We focus on making "converts to a particular faith and practice and baptize them into church membership," rather than leading them into discipleship of Jesus, "intent upon becoming Christ-like." Willard says, "This causes two great omissions from the Great Commission to stand out. Most important, we start by omitting the making of disciples and enrolling people as students, when we should let all else wait for that. Then, we also omit, of necessity, the step of taking our converts through training that will bring them ever-increasingly to do what Jesus directed." He later writes, "The cost of nondiscipleship is far greater—even when this life alone is considered—than the price paid to walk with Jesus, constantly learning from him."

Discipleship in the way of Jesus naturally produces great marriages and parenting, dynamic churches and communities, and attractive, fruitful lives, as we cannot live in the kingdom of God without loving others sacrificially, as Jesus modeled. I do not see how someone can look at scripture and not conclude that obedience to Christ's teachings is the foundation to living in faith.

To become fruit producers, we must learn to disciple ourselves and others as Jesus did. That is the only soil that produces thirtyfold, sixtyfold, and hundredfold lives of eternal wealth. We must strive together to be a spiritual community that is united in this mission. Paul wrote to the Philippians, "Make my joy complete by being of the same mind, maintaining the same love, united in spirit, intent on one purpose. Have this attitude in yourselves which was also in Christ Jesus" (Philippians 2:2, 5 NASB). If Jesus self-proclaimed that his purpose was to bring about the kingdom of God, then maybe it should be our collective purpose too. We must agree on this, just as Paul wrote to the congregation in Philippi.

In A. W. Tozer's sermon "Unity That Brings Revival," he says, "Unity of mind precedes the blessings of God." He went on to express that "unity is necessary for the outpouring of the Holy Spirit." We should desire this, as the outpouring of the Holy Spirit is a requirement for experiencing the kingdom of God. "We should persist in the spirit of unity," he adds. This does not say we cannot have differences of opinion or doctrine or that our own personalities and giftedness cannot be applied in our kingdom experience, but we all must abide in Jesus and remain in unity of mind and spirit.

Dr. Mark Labberton, president of Fuller Seminary, recently shared a speech titled "The Crisis of Evangelicalism and Fake Good News" at a summit for evangelical leaders at Wheaton College in Chicago. He said,

> Only the Spirit "who is in the world to convict us of sin and righteousness and judgment" (John 16:8) can bring us to clarity about the crisis we face [in evangelical Christian culture]. As I have sought that conviction, here is what I have come to believe: the central crisis facing us is that the gospel

of Jesus Christ has been betrayed and shamed by an evangelicalism that has violated its own moral and spiritual integrity. This is not a crisis imposed from outside the household of faith, but from within.

Dr. Labberton and other evangelical leaders share my frustration with the gradual distortion of the gospel of Jesus. This is a by-product of compromise, over time, from Christian leaders who seek power, wealth, and influence in the way of the world, rather than the way Jesus commanded. Before Jesus began his ministry, he went into the wilderness to fast and be tempted by Satan. These temptations that he overcame were the exact things that Christianity today does not overcome. Jesus rejected the temptation to abuse his power or compromise his purpose in order to receive all the wealth and influence of this world, as offered by the enemy. Jesus knew this would one day all be his, but he had a greater mission than self. He came to bring about the kingdom of God, and it operates completely different from our worldly system.

Jesus used the process of apprenticeship to teach his disciples about leading in his kingdom. Becoming multipliers in the kingdom requires leadership that models Christ. This is all dependent on knowing the gospel of Jesus and never letting go of it. We never outgrow our need for the gospel. It is not just the message we heard to come to Christ or that we believed so we would be saved. It is our lifeblood for living daily in the kingdom of God as we are transformed into the likeness of Jesus.

We must never forget the gospel is a person—Jesus, Immanuel, God with us. We cannot separate him from his message and purpose, which is the kingdom of God. This must be our message, our good news, and we must persist in advancing our way into it collectively.

Let us all remember this: one cannot proclaim the Gospel of Jesus without the tangible witness of one's life.

—Pope Francis

LENS CHANGES

Very little is known about Jesus's life prior to his baptism. We have accounts of his birth in Matthew and Luke, and from those two books, we know his genealogy. We also have several prophecies recorded that were told to his parents, and we read that Mary and Joseph fled with him to Egypt to avoid Herod's slaughter of male babies. After his earliest months, the only story of him prior to his baptism is when he was twelve. On a family trip to Jerusalem for the Feast of the Passover, Jesus accidentally was left behind. He was found three days later (this makes me feel so much better as a parent), hanging out in the temple, sitting among the teachers, listening and asking questions. "All who heard Him were amazed at His understanding and His answers" (Luke 2:47 NASB).

His response to his mother when she finally found him was, "Did you not know that I had to be in My Father's house?" (Luke 2:49 NASB).

This account of Jesus is all we know of what he was like as a child. Clearly, he had a unique understanding and interest in the affairs of his heavenly Father, but we know nothing of the next eighteen years of his life, with the exception of Luke noting, "Jesus kept increasing in wisdom and stature, and in favor with God and men" (Luke 2:52 NASB). Only after Jesus began his public ministry do we find a reference in Mark 6:3 that he was a builder by trade. (The Greek word *tekton* means builder or artisan, which could mean he was a carpenter, but more likely, because of the region, he was a stonemason.)

This brings us to where the real story of Jesus of Nazareth begins in the Gospels—at his baptism. Though the miraculous virgin birth is noteworthy, Mark and John do not mention anything about his life prior to his baptism by his cousin John. This event is where they choose to start telling their accounts of Jesus. In my assessment of scripture, it is the most significant event, next to his death and resurrection, in all of scripture, as it is emphasized in all four Gospels.

Mark's Gospel begins with John the Baptist ministering in the wilderness with the purpose of making "ready the way of the Lord" (Mark 1:3 NASB). John said to those to whom he was preaching, "I baptized you with water; but He will baptize you with the Holy Spirit" (Mark 1:8 NASB).

When Jesus appears on the scene, he is unknown to the crowd, and he asks John to baptize him. John did not feel worthy to do so, but Jesus replied, "Permit it at this time; for in this way it is fitting for us to fulfill all righteousness" (Matthew 3:15 NASB). So John baptized Jesus. "Immediately coming up out of the water, He saw the heavens opening, and the Spirit like a dove descending upon Him; and a voice came out of the heavens: 'You are My beloved Son, in You I am well-pleased.' Immediately the Spirit impelled Him to go out into the wilderness" (Mark 1:10–12 NASB). There, he fasted for forty days and faced the temptations of Satan before returning to begin his ministry.

We do not know enough about Jesus prior to this moment to know if the Holy Spirit dwelled in him before his baptism, but we do know that all four Gospel writers noted that the Holy Spirit visibly descended upon him at this time. The Gospel of John records that John the Baptist acknowledged that it remained upon him (John 1:33). This is groundbreaking for the new covenant and the kingdom of God to come about.

In the old covenant, the Holy Spirit came upon man, but

because of sin, he could not dwell forever. As I have heard it said by Pastor Graham Cooke, "We went from a visitational culture to a habitational culture," as it pertains to our relationship with the Holy Spirit. This, of course, did not happen for anyone else for about three years, until the day of Pentecost after Jesus ascended to heaven, but it set an important precedent that was necessary for righteousness.

Because Christ "did not regard equality with God a thing to be grasped, but [laid aside His privileges], taking the form of a bond-servant, and being made in the likeness of men" (Philippians 2:6–7), Jesus modeled dependency on the Holy Spirit to us. He showed us what it looks like to submit to the will of his Father in heaven. Jesus said, "The Son can do nothing of Himself, unless it is something He sees the Father doing; for whatever the Father does, these things the Son also does in like manner. For I did not speak on My own initiative, but the Father Himself who sent Me has given Me a commandment as to what to say and what to speak" (John 5:19, 12:49 NASB).

Unhindered by sin, Jesus saw the will of God with perfect clarity. Therefore, he was able to make God known to the world. As Jesus prayed at the Last Supper, "I have manifested Your [character] to the men whom You gave Me out of the world … Now they have come to know that everything You gave Me I have given them" (John 17:6 NASB).

Even though Jesus revealed God to his disciples, it was not until they were filled with the Holy Spirit that they began to walk and grow in the kingdom of God and experience lens changes. Though they received the Holy Spirit in an instant, their clarity of God's will was unveiled progressively. Despite Jesus's having told them before his ascension into heaven, "You will receive power when the Holy Spirit has come upon you; and you shall be my witnesses both in Jerusalem, and in all Judea and Samaria, and even to the remotest part of the earth" (Acts 1:8 NASB), it was several years before any of them went out from Jerusalem and began to truly obey the great commission. Neither should we expect perfect obedience upon receiving the Holy Spirit; we should expect only a journey to completion.

Lens changes are the *aha* moments, where we see something that God is up to that we could not see before. It is evident throughout Acts and Paul's epistles that even the earliest followers of Jesus were not fully enlightened in the instant they received the Holy Spirit.

- It took roughly seven years before Peter was given a vision that it was okay for him to enter a Gentile's house, eat unclean food, and convert and baptize a non-Jew. This was unwelcome news at first to the rest of the believers, until they agreed with Peter that it was a good thing, saying, "Well then, God has granted to the Gentiles also the repentance that leads to life" (Acts 11:18 NASB).
- Not until the Jerusalem Council, estimated to be eighteen years after Pentecost, did the leaders of the church come to agreement that it was not necessary for Gentiles to be circumcised or to direct them to observe the Law of Moses (Acts 15:5).
- While on his second missionary journey, Paul was traveling through Asia with Silas and Timothy, but the Holy Spirit did not permit them to speak the Word there. They desired to go to another neighboring region called Bithynia, but the Spirit of Jesus did not permit them to go. Despite their good intentions, God had other plans that were not always known to them.
- It is believed Paul wrote 2 Corinthians in AD 57, roughly twenty-three years after his conversion; in this letter, he writes of a "thorn in the flesh, a messenger of Satan" that tormented him. Paul mentions that he implored the Lord three times to make it leave him but later received the following words from the Lord: "My grace is sufficient for you, for power is perfected in weakness" (2 Corinthians 12:9

NASB). Something that Paul once saw as an affliction he eventually saw as a blessing.

- In Philippians we read that what was once considered of great value to Paul—his worldly and religious credentials—he eventually considered as garbage "in view of the surpassing value of knowing Christ Jesus my Lord." He went on to write, "Let us therefore, as many as are [being perfected] have this attitude; and if in anything you [are otherwise minded], God will reveal that also to you" (Philippians 3:8, 15 NASB).

We must expect and embrace the process of lens changes in order that we may grow in Christ. We must never settle for where we are or what we already think we know of God. He has so much more in store for you and me.

Are you asking God for a lens change?

Eyes to See the Kingdom

Jesus's desire for his disciples is that we will see the kingdom of God just as he did. As mentioned earlier, Jesus depended on the Holy Spirit to do and say all that his heavenly Father willed. We often forget that Jesus was fully man while he walked this earth and "that he did not regard equality with God a thing to be grasped" (Philippians 2:6 NASB).

Jesus often retreated into isolation and prayer. He cherished his alone time with his Father for connection. In these times, removed from activity and distraction, Jesus was able to receive perfect clarity on what the Father willed him to say and do. By giving up his divine privileges, Jesus was able to model to us what dependence on God looks like. The Sermon on the Mount begins with the message that we are blessed when we depend on God, for in our dependence is the kingdom of Heaven (Matthew 5:3 paraphrased).

Jesus did not come to start a religion that would give us access to heaven when we die; rather, he came to bring heaven to earth. "He who descended is Himself also He who ascended far above all the heavens, so that He might fill all things" (Ephesians 4:10 NASB). This should be our desire.

Jesus taught his disciples to pray, "Your kingdom come. Your will be done, on earth as it is in heaven" (Matthew 6:10 NASB). Jesus was and still is spreading the way of heaven on earth, and we are his method for doing so. God "gave Him as head over all things to the [church], which is His body, the fullness of Him who fills all in all" (Ephesians 1:23 NASB). We have been invited to be ministry partners with Jesus, ambassadors of his kingdom. We were brought into the body of Christ with one missional purpose—to disciple all people into the character of God in order that we may be multipliers of the kingdom of God, receiving all that God desires to give us so that we may give it away. However, we cannot give what we do not possess. We cannot pour out his living water if we are not full of it.

This starts with knowing God, not just knowing *about* God. I knew all about God and looked more like a Pharisee in my youth and young adult years than I looked like Jesus. The evangelical Christian Pharisee looks much like the individuals Paul was rebuking in Corinth when he wrote, "If I ... do not have [God's] love, I have become a noisy gong or a clanging cymbal" (1 Corinthians 13:1 NASB). This came after he had written, "For the kingdom of God does not consist in words but in power" (1 Corinthians 4:20 NASB). Most lifelong Christians do not need more knowledge about God or how to share with others what they believe; rather, they need to know the power of God intimately. It is hard to argue with personal experience.

This starts with the recognition of one's brokenness. The problem is that we want to be made complete without being broken. As Jesus brought to the attention of the Pharisees, we are all broken; they just did a better job of covering it up culturally and within their religious system than the "sinners" did. Without authentic, transparent leadership in our congregations, we will remain broken men and women, trying to work out our own issues by ourselves. As Kyle Idleman puts it in his book *The End of Me: Where Real Life in the Upside-Down Ways of Jesus Begins*, "The greatest danger in life is anything other than Jesus that becomes a foundation for our confidence. Performance-based religion is the false foundation of choice for many of us who grew up in the church."

When we come to faith we are "born again," but often we never are allowed to be the infants that we are in the way of Jesus. As a parent of two young boys, I understand the capabilities of newborns—they mostly eat, sleep, poop, and cry. (We think they can smile, but that's really just gas.)

One day my wife was bragging on our son for rolling over for the first time. I did not realize that was such a big accomplishment. Then, eventually, he learned to crawl, walk, talk, run, and play. (I promised my wife in the early years that I would be a much better father once they could play sports.) This took time. Some things came naturally to them, but most things were learned through instruction, observation, and imitation. The playing does not happen until one develops all the other foundational elements. Most often, we do not give the grace and foundations required to follow Jesus to a new believer that we give our babies. We expect nothing of an infant, and neither does God expect anything of one who has just been born again spiritually.

Christian culture, however, tells new believers how they are to conduct themselves from the very beginning, expecting them to walk in maturity from day one. This is how performance-based religion begins. New believers must be nurtured in the way of Jesus with a healthy balance of support and challenge, but we should first err on the side of support. We must help new believers pick up their broken pieces and teach them how to let Jesus put them together to work properly in his kingdom. His desire is to teach us how to play and thrive in the kingdom of God.

Most churches today fail to teach new believers how to grow in dependence on Christ; instead, we teach them all about the Bible and our doctrine, and we emphasize good Christian performance. We spoon-feed head knowledge and do very little equipping for spiritual transformation. We do not model what it looks like to repent from the ways of the world to follow Jesus. Perhaps that is because most "mature Christians" have never done it themselves. Many Christians have never seen or advanced into the kingdom of God, so it should not be a surprise that it is not given away.

Jesus's purpose was to proclaim, teach, and model the kingdom of God. He was the only one who knew it intimately. As the disciple John wrote, "And the Word became flesh, and dwelt among us, and we saw His glory, glory as of the only begotten from the Father, full of grace and truth … grace and truth were realized through Jesus Christ. No one has seen God at any time; the only begotten God who is in the bosom of the Father, He has explained Him" (John 1:14, 17b–18 NASB).

John and the other disciples offer testimony to what God's coming to earth looks like. This is the part of the kingdom of God that is at hand. Jesus manifested the character of God to his disciples so that they could see what his will was for his children and how they should live in obedience to their Creator and Lord. They were granted the privilege of seeing God's kingdom lived out on earth, and nothing could stop them from spreading it once they had it in them.

Jesus said to his disciples, "To you it has been granted to know the mysteries of the kingdom of God, but to the rest it is in parables"— then, quoting the prophet Isaiah—"so that 'seeing they may not see, and hearing they may not understand'" (Luke 8:10 NASB). Discipleship of Jesus is necessary for living in God's kingdom. We are commissioned to make disciples, and we must disciple ourselves so that we may disciple others.

Jesus's most commonly quoted phrase is, "He who has ears to hear, let him hear." His desire is for us to know and understand that which he knew intimately about the Father. This is what Paul learned to value more than his knowledge of scripture or any of his religious credentials.

> But whatever things were gain to me, those things I have counted as loss for the sake of Christ. More than that, I count all things to be loss in view of the surpassing value of knowing Christ Jesus my Lord, for whom I have suffered the loss of all things, and count them but rubbish so that I may gain Christ, and may be found in Him, not having a righteousness of my own derived from the Law, but that which is through faith in Christ, the righteousness which comes from God on the basis of faith, that I may know Him and the power of His resurrection and the fellowship of His sufferings. (Philippians 3:7–10a NASB)

Paul uses an interesting word here for "knowing" Jesus. He does not use the Greek word that would represent the knowledge of facts; rather, he uses the word *gnoseos*, which implies experiential knowledge. It's often used to describe the knowledge, inside and out, that one has of a spouse. Paul valued this above anything else, and so should we. It should be our desire to know Jesus more intimately and experientially than anything else. After all, we were created through him and designed to be in him. "Even as You, Father, are in Me and I in You, that they also may be in Us" (John 17:21 NASB).

If we are to be "in Jesus," then we must get to know God personally and intimately:

- This is eternal life, that they may know You, the only true God, and Jesus Christ whom You have sent. (John 17:3)
- For this reason also, since the day we heard of it, we have not ceased to pray for you and to ask that you may be filled with the knowledge of His will in all spiritual wisdom and

understanding, so that you will walk in a manner worthy of the Lord, to please Him in all respects, bearing fruit in every good work and increasing in the knowledge of God. (Colossians 1:9–10)

- That the God of our Lord Jesus Christ, the Father of glory, may give to you a spirit of wisdom and of revelation in the knowledge of Him. I pray that the eyes of your heart may be enlightened, so that you will know what is the hope of His calling, what are the riches of the glory of His inheritance in the saints. (Ephesians 1:17–18)

- So that Christ may dwell in your hearts through faith; and that you, being rooted and grounded in love, may be able to comprehend with all the saints what is the breadth and length and height and depth, and to know the love of Christ which surpasses knowledge, that you may be filled up to all the fullness of God. (Ephesians 3:17–19)

- That their hearts may be encouraged, having been knit together in love, and attaining to all the wealth that comes from the full assurance of understanding, resulting in a true knowledge of God's mystery, that is, Christ Himself. (Colossians 2:2)

- We are destroying speculations and every lofty thing raised up against the knowledge of God, and we are taking every thought captive to the obedience of Christ. (2 Corinthians 10:5)

- Beloved, let us love one another, for love is from God; and everyone who loves is born of God and knows God. The one who does not love does not know God, for God is love. (1 John 4:7–8 NASB)

True knowledge of God does not come academically with more information; rather, it is gained through experience of walking in faith. As we walk with him and experience his love and grace, we gain more knowledge of who he is and how he works. As the mysteries of

God become more understood, we begin to see things through his eternal lens. These progressive revelations are lens changes, and they only happen when we turn areas of our lives over to him. When we hold on to the things and ways of this world, we remain blind to the kingdom of God.

When we receive the Holy Spirit, we do not automatically gain 20/20 vision of God's Kingdom; we just gain access. We receive the key to the kingdom, but the key only works for the doors for which our spiritual maturity level is ready. Only God knows what you are ready for, and he wants to give it to you; he is often simply more patient than we are. Remember, a student is not above his teacher, but every disciple, once fully trained, will become like his teacher. Jesus desires maturity for us, but he must do it progressively and often slower than we would like. Jesus said, "Therefore you are to be [brought to maturity], as your heavenly Father is [complete]" (Matthew 5:48 NASB).

Many translations use the word *perfect*, but this does not make the most sense in context, especially considering that two different Greek words are used in the manuscripts. The first is *teleioi*, and although it can mean perfect, it is better translated as complete or mature. In the natural sense, teleioi are adults who have attained their full stature, strength, and mental powers; they have attained their goal (*telos*). The second word used to describe God's character is *teleios*. This is the end goal; this is the completion or perfection for which we are striving.

The process is addressed later in the Sermon on the Mount.

> Ask, and it will be given to you; seek, and you will find; knock, and it will be opened to you. For everyone who asks receives, and he who seeks finds, and to him who knocks it will be opened. Or what man is there among you who, when his son asks for a loaf, will give him a stone? Or if he asks for a fish, he will not give him a snake, will he? If you then,

being evil, know how to give good gifts to your children, how much more will your Father who is in heaven give what is good to those who ask Him! (Matthew 7:7–11 NASB)

Our heavenly Father wants to release all of heaven to us, but this takes effort on our part. This is where our active participation comes into play; we have work to do. We must ask for it, seek it out, and knock on the doors that we want God to open. This is where God's grace is poured out on us. As Dallas Willard wrote in *The Great Omission*,

> Learning Christ-likeness is not passive. It is active engagement with and in God. And we act with our bodies … the use and training of the body is the place where faith meets grace to achieve conformity. Grace is not opposed to effort, it is opposed to earning. Earning is an attitude. Effort is an action. Grace, you know, does not just have to do with forgiveness of sins alone.

Grace is everything that God pours out in our direction so that we may walk and grow with him and partner in his work. Grace is applied for us to come into relationship with him, and grace is continually poured out on us as we grow into his likeness.

We can do nothing on our own to earn God's grace, but we certainly should strive toward completion. This is exactly what Paul was referring to when he wrote, "Not that I have already obtained it or have already become perfect, but I press on so that I may lay hold of that for which also I was laid hold of by Christ Jesus. Brethren, I do not regard myself as having laid hold of it yet; but one thing I do: forgetting what lies behind and reaching forward to what lies ahead, I press on toward the goal for the prize of the upward call of God in Christ Jesus" (Philippians 3:12–14 NASB). He also wrote in the same letter, "For it is God who is at work in you, both to will and to work for His good pleasure" (Philippians 2:13 NASB).

God wants us to be engaged in his work in us and through us. Remember, we cannot give away what we do not possess, so we must always ask God for learning opportunities. Some of these may come at a cost. Are you willing to give up the world to inherit the kingdom of God?

Jesus said, "The kingdom of heaven is like a treasure hidden in the field, which man found and hid again; and from joy over it he goes and sells all that he has and buys that field" (Matthew 13:44 NASB). This is what happens when we begin to experience kingdom lens changes. We see God doing things that we never could see before. We begin to have paradigm shifts in our thinking. The seemingly upside-down kingdom of God eventually appears more real than does the kingdom of this world. The goal is to get to the point where we feel like aliens in a foreign land. We recognize that our citizenship is in heaven and not in this world. The eternal becomes more important to us than the temporal, which is decaying.

I wrote in a previous chapter that my life verse is Romans 12:2: "Do not conform to the pattern of this world, but be transformed by the renewing of your mind, so that you may prove what the will of God is, that which is good and acceptable and perfect" (NASB).

Maturing us into the perfection of his Son and to seeing the way of his kingdom does not happen overnight; it is a process. The word used for transformation in the Greek text is *metamorphousthe*. This is where we get the word *metamorphosis*—a change of the form or nature of a thing or person into a completely different one, by natural or supernatural means.

We are familiar with this process when a caterpillar becomes a butterfly, but we often miss that we were meant to be transformed from a larva to a beautiful flying being in the kingdom of God. This process is done through the renewing of our minds. We must learn to think differently so we can see what God is doing in the world around us. He wants us to be engaged in his work, but it requires lens changes. We must stop doing things in the manner of the world and stop depending on our own capabilities and talents. All the while, we must see ourselves as the butterflies that he sees us as, rather than the struggling larva that cultural Christianity often wants to make us believe we still are.

UPSIDE DOWN

Jesus answered, "My kingdom is not of this world. If My kingdom were of this world, then My servants would be fighting so that I would not be handed over to the Jews; but as it is, My kingdom is not of this realm."

—John 18:36 (NASB)

But many who are first will be last; and the last, first.

—Matthew 19:30 (NASB)

Looking back throughout my Christian education and church-attending life, I was taught very little in the way of the kingdom of God. Instead, I was and continue to be taught in the way of the American dream—prosperity, capitalism, and conservative values, to all be applied with a "Christian worldview." This is not unique to just one of my church experiences.

Throughout my life, I have attended small and large Methodist, Baptist, Church of God, Presbyterian, and nondenominational churches, and though there were differences in style of worship, doctrine, formalities, and liturgical practices, very little emphasis ever was placed on the kingdom of God, as Jesus taught.

The way of Jesus is often forsaken and unknown in most churches and Christian segments. The American way of life and the kingdom of God are seemingly at odds, and so Christian culture has adopted a hybrid faith in order to accommodate the values. If we want to advance into the kingdom of God, we must truly examine Jesus's teachings and understand that he was not establishing a new religious doctrine or overarching principles by which to live our lives. He commands us to obey so that we may live in his kingdom that is not of this world.

Following Jesus is not about intellectual ascent; it is a change of the direction of our lives.

"And you know the way where I am going," Jesus said to his disciples. Then Thomas replied, "Lord, we do not know where You are going, how do we know the way?" Jesus said to him, "I am the way, and the truth, and the life; no one comes to the Father but through Me. If you had known Me, you would have known My Father also; from now on you know Him, and have seen Him" (John 14:4–7 NASB).

Christianity has used John 14:6 as a doctrinal claim for exclusive access to heaven when we die, but Jesus was making a directional claim. Following Jesus is not about believing he was the Messiah and simply asking for a once-and-for-all forgiveness of sin because of his death and resurrection. It is a way of life. It is living the kingdom life, which is the direction of heaven. It requires obedience to what he taught.

Andy Stanley's book *The Principle of the Path* is about "how to get from where you are to where you want to be." It is based on the principle that "direction, not desire, determines destination." He emphasizes that we are all going to end up somewhere, so we probably should determine where we want to end up and set our direction accordingly.

If the good news of Jesus was the kingdom of God, and it was the emphasis of his teachings, then his kingdom should be the destination to which we set the course of our lives. When teaching in Atlanta, I often use the following illustration: If I want to take my family on a vacation to Disney World, there is only one interstate and one direction I can take out of Atlanta to get there. I must get on I-75 South. I could take I-75 North, I-85, or I-20 in either direction, or I could drive around in circles on I-285, but unless I take I-75 South, I'm not going to get where I want to go. This sounds like common sense, but thoughtfully examine your life and faith. Are you heading in the direction Jesus taught and established as *the way*?

> Therefore everyone who hears these words of mine and puts them into practice is like a wise man who built his house on the rock. The rain came down, the streams rose, and the winds blew and beat against that house; yet it did not fall, because it had its foundation on the rock. But everyone who hears these words of mine and does not put them into practice is like a foolish man who built his house on sand. The rain came down, the streams rose, and the winds blew and beat against that house, and it fell with a great crash. (Matthew 7:24–27 NASB)

Are you taking his words seriously and putting them into practice?

Jesus said, "If you love Me, you will keep My commandments" (John 14:15 NASB). Many cultural Christians say they love Jesus, but I find very little leadership into obedience of what he actually commanded. However, let us first look at that which Jesus refused to accept so that we can understand the direction of the kingdom of God in which Jesus is leading us.

I think we often overlook some foundational insights to the kingdom of God in the accounts of Jesus's temptations in the wilderness. He established a significant precedent for his kingdom in denying these temptations from Satan. We often dismiss their significance to our understanding the characteristics of living in the kingdom.

In hindsight, we say, "Of course Jesus was not going to sell his soul to the devil and take Satan up on his temptations." However, have you ever thought about the significance of what he gave up? Or more important, do you consider the ways that you are compromising your soul by giving in to these very same temptations?

Immediately after his baptism,

> Jesus was led up by the Spirit into the wilderness to be tempted by the devil. And after He had fasted forty days and forty nights, He then became hungry. [Possibly the most obvious statement in the Bible!] And the tempter came and said to Him, "If You are the Son of God, command that these stones become bread." But He answered and said, "It is written, 'Man shall not live on bread alone, but on every word that proceeds out of the mouth of God.'" (Matthew 4:1–4 NASB)

As a fully human being, not a superhero, Jesus obviously was very hungry and certainly desired food after fasting for forty days. He was being tempted to take control of the situation by using the power that he had to fix the temporary situation of hunger. It is important to see that Jesus understood and set an example that in his kingdom, man does not rely on or abuse his own power. Instead, in the kingdom of God, man depends on God for everything.

> Then the devil took Him into the holy city and had Him stand on the pinnacle of the temple, and said to Him, "If You are the Son of God, throw Yourself down; for it is written, 'He will command His angels concerning You'; and 'On their hands they will bear You up, so that You will not strike Your foot against a stone.'" Jesus said to him, "On the other hand, it is written, 'You shall not put the Lord your God to the test.'" (Matthew 4:5–7 NASB)

Jesus, being the Son of God, knew that he could ask anything of the Father, and it would be granted. He knew the influence he had over the angels and that he could obligate his Father to come through for him, but he refused to use his influence for his own gratification. In the kingdom of God, influence is not used for one's own benefit.

> Again, the devil took Him to a very high mountain and showed Him all the kingdoms of the world and their glory; and he said to Him, "All these things I will give You, if You fall down and worship me." Then Jesus said to him, "Go, Satan! For it is written, 'You shall worship the Lord your God, and serve Him only.'" (Matthew 4:8–10 NASB)

Everything the world had to offer was being offered to Jesus. Satan offered him all the wealth of the world—it would one day be his, but he could take a shortcut to it. He would not have to go through the trials and persecution and, ultimately, death on a cross to have it. Satan was willing to offer it immediately if Jesus would simply make a compromise to God's plan. However, Jesus refused because he saw with clarity the wondrous beauty of the everlasting kingdom of God that was promised to him. In the kingdom of God, worldly wealth does not compare to the riches that are to come.

How does this impact us?

Jesus set the stage for the kingdom of God with nobody watching. He chose not to abuse power, influence, and wealth for self-interest and to deny himself of it all to make available his future kingdom for mankind. The kingdom of God operates upside down from the kingdom of this world, and Jesus knew his role was to model the way of God to man.

In his sermon series *Ninety*, Andy Stanley said that Jesus taught us:

- Power is not primarily for the benefit of the powerful.
- Wealth is not primarily for the benefit of the wealthy.
- Influence is not primarily for the benefit of the influential.

The kingdom of God is the opposite of the kingdoms of this world. In the kingdom of God, power, wealth, and influence benefits others, not self.

> "For what does it profit a man to gain the whole world, and forfeit his soul?" (Mark 8:36 NASB)

Phariseeism, whether in ancient Judaism or modern-day Christianity, has emerged as the common religious practice. It is nothing more than pursuing the direction of the world in a religious way. It is selfish in nature. It teaches its adherents to use power, influence, and wealth for personal and collective benefit within the parameters of certain rules. Religion teaches us, without saying it directly, that we can obligate God to reward us for our "good behavior" and our ability to check the boxes that we believe are most important.

> "But go and learn what this means: 'I desire compassion, and not sacrifice,' for I did not come to call the [self-righteous], but sinners." (Matthew 9:13 NASB)

The kingdom of God is not for the religious or the self-righteous; rather, it is for the poor in spirit, the broken, and the sick—the ones who know they are dependent on God. This is not the way of the world.

The Counter-Cultural, Upside-Down Kingdom

The Sermon on the Mount begins with what we call the Beatitudes:

"Blessed are the poor in spirit, for theirs is the kingdom of heaven." (Not: Blessed are the self-determined, independent, and confident.)

"Blessed are those who mourn, for they shall be comforted." (Not: Blessed are those who put on the perfect show.)

"Blessed are the gentle, for they shall inherit the earth." (Not: Blessed are those who prosper through shrewd business deals and advantageous contracts.)

"Blessed are those who hunger and thirst for righteousness, for they shall be satisfied." (Not: Blessed are those who seek gratification, for they will be satisfied.)

"Blessed are the merciful, for they shall receive mercy." (Not: God takes care of those who take care of themselves.)

"Blessed are the pure in heart, for they shall see God." (Not: Blessed are the strict religious adherents.)

"Blessed are the peacemakers, for they shall be called sons of God." (Not: Blessed are those who love only those who treat them well.)

"Blessed are those who have been persecuted for the sake of righteousness, for theirs is the kingdom of heaven." (Not: Blessed are those who have made a personal commitment of faith.)

"Blessed are you when people insult you and persecute you, and falsely say all kinds of evil against you because of Me." (Not: Blessed are you when life goes smoothly and without trials.)

Rejoice and be glad, for your reward in heaven is great; for in the same way they persecuted the prophets who were before you. (Matthew 5:12)

Entering the kingdom of God comes at a cost. The cost is self-interest. "He who loves his life loses it, and he who hates his life in this world will keep it to life eternal. If anyone serves Me, he must follow Me; and where I am, there My servant will be also; if anyone serves Me, the Father will honor him" (John 12:25–26 NASB).

Cultural Christianity has denied the cost of discipleship of Jesus. We have traded in Jesus and his kingdom for religious doctrine, self-reliant sin management, and human-derived practices.

In the Sermon on the Mount, Jesus continues to tell those who thought they were supposed to live exclusively from the rest of culture that they are to be a salt and light to the world. Evangelical Christianity embraces these verses but often misses the context in which they were given.

For fifteen hundred years, the nation of Israel was living an exclusionary lifestyle from all other cultures. They were not allowed to interact, eat with, worship, or do business with anyone outside of their own Jewish culture. Jesus taught something brand new to them. He drew a sharp contrast from the Law of Moses to the new way of the kingdom of God. He came to end the old covenant, which could not give life, and to usher in a new covenant, which could.

Jesus then said, "Do not think that I came to [demolish] the Law or the Prophets; I did not come to [demolish] but to fulfill ... not the smallest letter or stroke shall pass from the Law *until* all is accomplished" (Matthew 5:17–18, emphasis added). This is often misunderstood through a religious lens because we fail to understand that the kingdom of God Jesus was introducing was so much better than a new religious system. He was not enacting Judaism 2.0; rather, he was fulfilling the purpose of the Law and bringing forth the new covenant about which Jeremiah had prophesied would be so much better and placed in the hearts of man (Jeremiah 31:31–34).

This is where Jesus's last words on the cross have so much significance. Jesus had told his disciples just the night before, "I will not drink of the fruit of the vine, until the kingdom of God shall come" (Luke 22:16 KJV). In his final moments on the cross, John writes, "When Jesus had received the sour wine, He said, 'It is [accomplished]!' And bowed his head and gave up His spirit" (John 19:30 NASB).

Jesus accomplished all that was necessary to put the Law to death, fulfill the prophecies, and usher in the kingdom of God, just as he said he was doing. "The kingdom of God is not coming with signs to be observed; nor will they say, 'Look, here it is!' or, 'There it is!' For behold, the kingdom of God is [within you]" (Luke 17:20 NASB).

Paul put it this way in his letter to the Romans:

> For what the Law could not do, weak as it was through the flesh, God did: sending His own Son in the likeness of sinful flesh and as an offering for sin, He condemned sin in the flesh, so that the requirement of the Law might be fulfilled in us, who do not walk according to the flesh but according to the Spirit, the things of the Spirit. For the mind set on the flesh is death, but the mind set on the Spirit is life and peace. (Romans 8:3–6 NASB)

Life in the Spirit, which is the kingdom of God, does not live in the way of the world. It pursues that which is in the interest of others, which is the interest of God. "Truly I say to you, to the extent that you did it to one of these brothers of Mine, even the least of them, you did it to Me" (Matthew 25:40 NASB). Jesus modeled the love of God. He showed his disciples how to love others well and that it is not out of self-interest or to get something in return. We have one central purpose in the kingdom of God—to love.

> A new commandment I give to you, that you love one another, even as I have loved you, that you also love one another. By this all men will know that you are My disciples, if you have love for one another. (John 13:34–35 NASB)

Guaranteed Outcome

Now faith is the assurance of things hoped for, the
conviction of things not seen.

—Hebrews 11:1 (NASB)

The greatest challenge to walking fully in the kingdom of God is
the distractions of the kingdom of the world. We know we cannot
serve two masters, but we always will be tempted to serve and gratify
self. As we grow further into the kingdom of God, these desires will
diminish.

A disciple of Jesus cannot love the things of this world and Jesus.
Paradoxically, the culture of the kingdom of God is characterized
by loving the people of this world well. This summarizes all the
commandments that he has given us. Loving others is how we show
Jesus our love for him. He said, "If you love Me, you will keep My
commandments" (John 14:15 NASB).

We know that we will fall short in obedience at times. We will
trip up, but those instances should never define us or indicate a
different direction for our lives. Jesus is our direction. He is the Way.
He modeled God's love to us.

> Dear friends, let us love one another, for love comes
> from God. Everyone who loves has been born of
> God and knows God. This is how God showed
> his love among us: He sent his one and only Son

into the world that we might live through him … since God so loved us, we also ought to love one another. No one has ever seen God; but if we love one another, God lives in us and his love is made complete in us. He has given us of his Spirit … God lives in them and they in God. And so we know and rely on the love God has for us.

God is love. Whoever lives in love lives in God, and God in them. This is how love is made complete among us so that we will have confidence on the day of judgment: In this world we are like Jesus. There is no fear in love. But perfect love drives out fear, because fear has to do with punishment. The one who fears is not made perfect in love. (1 John 4:7, 9, 11–13, 16–18 NIV)

We know to what we have been called. We know what Jesus is in the process of perfecting in us. As followers of Jesus, the only way for us to finish the course of life in submissive obedience to Jesus is by focusing on the glorious outcome that he has guaranteed us. Without a vision of our end goal, we inevitably will drift in purpose and mission.

We will get distracted by the temptations of the world.

We will settle for where we already are.

We will stop running the race.

Brothers and sisters, I do not consider myself yet to have taken hold of it. But one thing I do: Forgetting what is behind and straining toward what is ahead, I press on toward the goal to win the prize for which God has called me heavenward in Christ Jesus. (Philippians 3:13–14 NIV)

As a competitive golfer, one of the keys to executing great shots is envisioning the ball going where you want it to go before you ever hit the shot. It is also necessary that you put the past behind and focus only on the what is in front of you. As a Jesus apprentice, we should do the same. We must envision the end goal to which God has called us. The end goal is our new starting place.

This falls right in line with Stephen Covey's *The 7 Habits of Highly Effective People.* Habit 2: Begin with the end in mind. The renowned author and speaker says this habit "is based on imagination—the ability to envision in your mind what you cannot at present see with your eyes." He goes on to say that all things are created twice—a mental creation and a physical creation. "The physical creation follows the mental, just as a building follows a blueprint."

When God created you, he designed you with an end goal in mind, with a blueprint.

Being called to Christ means that we are predestined to become conformed to the image of Jesus. When we commit to follow Jesus, we are called into discipleship of Jesus to learn to become like him. We are called into a transformational process. This is the life journey that has been set before us—to seek transformation into his likeness. In his likeness, we see things from an eternal perspective rather than a worldly one. We understand that "there is now no condemnation for those who are in Christ Jesus" (Romans 8:1 NASB), and we live in victory.

Victory is our starting place!

> And we know that God causes all things to work together for good to those who love God, to those who are called according to His purpose. For those whom He foreknew, He also predestined to become conformed to the image of His Son, so that He would be the firstborn among many brethren; and these whom He predestined, He also called; and these whom He called, He also justified; and these

whom He justified, He also glorified. What then shall we say to these things? If God is for us, who is against us? He who did not spare His own Son, but delivered Him over for us all, how will He not also with Him freely give us all things? (Romans 8:28–31 NASB)

If this is our guarantee, then what is keeping us from confidently advancing into the kingdom of God?

The kingdom of this world is our only hindrance—the lure of worldly success and wealth and the distraction of pain and trials. In this life, we will have struggles. Jesus did not support any other contradictory thought to that, but he promises to be our solution. "In this world you will have many trials and sorrows. But take heart, because I have overcome the world" (John 16:33 NLT). Only he can bring us true freedom.

Any belief that causes you to feel that God is absent during your trials is not from above. The enemy wants you to believe that you are not in God's favor if you are struggling or not experiencing worldly success. This is a trap of Phariseeism, and it has seeped into cultural Christianity.

This is not part of Jesus's gospel. Prosperity gospel and following Jesus are often in complete juxtaposition. This is not because God does not want blessings for you. It is because he cares more about his end goal for you than making you comfortable or freeing you from a temporary trial that he may be using for your spiritual growth.

Remember, he has a plan!

Jesus came to free us from the bondage of this world, not to free us from its difficulties. He knows the enemy uses pain and suffering to distract us, and he offers us hope that it will not last.

When we keep our eyes focused on the temporal rather than the eternal, we allow our hope to be defeated. Satan uses our pain and struggles, as well as using faulty religious teachings that link success and prosperity in this world with God. He does this to take our eyes off the prize of our heavenly calling.

The purpose of this book has been to teach you through my own spiritual journey by being as transparent as possible. I understand how easy it is to trust worldly systems rather than God's way. We so often put more confidence in the flesh, in our own ability to change our circumstances, than in the Spirit. That is exactly why we must become apprentices of Jesus.

Following Jesus is a process. It is a lifetime of growth in the Spirit and a stripping away of the flesh.

We are all naturally wired to want to alleviate pain as quickly as possible. Paul offers us a great perspective on this:

> For I consider that the sufferings of this present time are not worthy to be compared with the glory that is to be revealed to us. For the anxious longing of the creation waits eagerly for the revealing of the sons of God. For the creation was subjected to futility, not willingly, but because of Him who subjected it, in hope that the creation itself also will be set free from its slavery to corruption into the freedom of the glory of the children of God. For we know that the whole creation groans and suffers the pains of childbirth together until now. And not only this, but also we ourselves, having the first fruits of the Spirit, even we ourselves groan within ourselves, waiting eagerly for our adoption as sons, the redemption of our body. For in hope we have been saved, but hope that is seen is not hope; for who hopes for what he already sees? But if we hope for what we do not see, with perseverance we wait eagerly for it. (Romans 8:18–25 NASB)

Paul's perspective grew into an eternal one through his submission to Jesus. It is easier said than done, and it is not something you can simply read one time and hope to own it in your thinking. It takes persistence and determination, along with abiding in Jesus, to become like him.

Nothing in our DNA embraces pain and suffering. We have the natural instincts of fight or flight, not to pursue trials. However, if we are honest, it is in the trials of life that we grow the most.

We rarely grow in our ease, comfort, or prosperity.

Bill Eckstrom, President of the Ecsell Institute, says in his TED Talk, "What makes you comfortable can ruin you, and only in a state of discomfort can you continually grow." (TEDx University of Nevada, January 21, 2017)

If I asked you to tell me about the times in your life when you grew the most, you would likely tell me that it was during a trial. And if I asked you if you desired to grow more, you of course would say, "Yes."

So why do you not seek more trials in your life?

Naturally, it is because you don't like the pain that comes with them. I don't either. We do, however, like the growth! Right?

It is through personal determination to grow into the being that I believe God intended when creating me that I strive and press on. I will continue to learn more of Jesus and eventually own it.

We all have areas of scripture that we struggle with; they even can cause doubt in our faith. For me, one of these passages is in the epistle of James. It opens with an incredibly challenging piece of scripture that took me a long time to reconcile. He writes, "Consider it all joy, my brethren, when you encounter various trials, knowing that the testing of your faith produces endurance. And let endurance have its perfect result, so that you may be perfect and complete, lacking in nothing" (James 1:2–4 NASB).

I know God wants to complete my journey to maturity, but do I really have to go through trials to get there?

There is nothing in my human way of thinking that naturally accepts this passage. I concluded, however, that if I could reach agreement with these difficult verses, then very little would be able to take my eyes off the kingdom of God.

How, though, could I see trials as a blessing from above?

This lesson presented itself to me in a season of life when I was battling some health issues that caused me great physical and emotional pain. My wife and I also had lost three close family members in a period of five months, and we were struggling financially. It seemed as if life was nothing but trials. I felt as if I had a bull's-eye on my back for Satan to take his shots. I sensed much weakness and vulnerability.

All I wanted was for God to fix the problems, but he had more in mind.

I asked God many times to intervene and remove my burdens. It even got to the point where I started asking God to just remove me from the world. I was in a pit of despair. But as much as I wanted out, it became clear to me that God had much more in store for me through my trials. He knew the promises he had made and the plans he had set. As much as I struggled during this difficult season, I refused to let go of the promises of the gospel.

At times I thought I was holding on to God, and he was ignoring me. I did not realize at that time that he remained closer to me than I ever knew. He was in the center of every circumstance, regardless of my faith.

It took me months of meditating on this passage, during the most trying period of life, before I could fully embrace the words God spoke through James. I cannot tell you exactly what happened. I just know the result.

I became convinced that the eternal prize for which God called me surpasses anything that is temporary. Even chronic pain in this life will be short-lived in the kingdom of God. And whatever makes me weak creates greater dependence on God. It draws me closer to him when I enter any circumstance with the end goal in mind.

I stopped asking God, "Why is this happening?" or "When are

you going to show up?" Instead, I started asking him, "What are you up to?" and "What is my role to play with you in this?"

I began to feel his joy in tough times, instead of my depression. I began to feel his peace amid the storms, instead of my worries. I started feeling thankful for what I had, rather than focusing on what was missing. I eventually saw what he already knew was on the other side of every situation I would face—an upgrade for me to become more like Jesus.

I do not believe God put the trials in my life. He was not testing my faith or gumption. I became convinced that his love for me as the perfect Father was too great to prevent more faith-building growth opportunities. In his sovereignty, he already saw the upgrade awaiting me on the other side, closer to his end goal for me.

This life is not easy. Following Jesus can be difficult at times, but he promises to finish what he starts. He knows what I need to be completed, so I don't need to persuade him that I know what is best. I just need to keep asking for his eyes to see what he already knows.

In case you were wondering, the trials have not stopped. Our finances are still not great. I continue to deal with some of my physical issues. The shots from the enemy keep coming, but I feel like I have gone through the training God sees as necessary for my next kingdom opportunity.

God has given me the very thing he promised when I turned from being a good Christian to following his Son—Jesus as my identity.

I discovered a gospel that cultural Christianity does not teach.

Granted, there is still so much more of God that I want to know. I certainly desire to keep growing in Christ. I have seen merely the tip of the iceberg in his kingdom. Nevertheless, I feel confident that I have discovered the true gospel of Jesus.

In the gospel of Jesus, we find the kingdom of God.

In the kingdom of God, we find all of God's promises.

In the promises of God, we find hope.

In hope, we find salvation.

In salvation, we find eternity.

In eternity, we have victory.

In victory, there is freedom.

In freedom, there is abundant life.

Nowhere in there do I find religion. So if you don't mind ... please stop calling me *Christian*.